I have always loved trains as they get you from one place to another, from one person to another, from one adventure to another. I even get a kick out of looking at empty railway lines disappearing into the narrowing, mysterious distance.

One of our teachers used to say to us, "If your life is a train journey, where are you going?" I thought he was mad. At the time I didn't know where I was going.

If life really *were* a train journey, I'd like to have interesting people around me for as long as the journey lasted – people like Jimmy Zest, Penelope Brown and the other quirky characters you'll meet in this story.

I hope you enjoy the antics of Zesty and his friends and, of course, your journey on Virgin Trains . . . wherever it takes you.

Sam McBratney

Also by Sam McBratney

Jimmy Zest

ZESTY

Sam McBratney

Illustrated by Tim Archbold

MACMILLAN CHILDREN'S BOOKS

First published 1982 by Hamish Hamilton Children's Books
This edition published in 2002 by Macmillan Children's Books
a division of Macmillan Publishers Limited
20 New Wharf Road, London N1 9RR
Basingstoke and Oxford
www.panmacmillan.com

In association with Virgin Trains

ISBN 0 330 39987 X

Text copyright © Sam McBratney 1982
Illustration copyright © Tim Archbold 2002

3 5 7 9 8 6 4

A CIP catalogue record for this book is available from the British Library.

Typeset by SX Composing DTP, Rayleigh, Essex
Printed and bound in Great Britain by Mackays of Chatham plc, Kent

Contents

- 1 -

Giant Money-boxes

Jimmy Zest was a born collector. He had collected egg boxes, badges, marbles, stamps, pebbles from the beach, key rings, comics, belemnites, things out of cereal packets – cereal packets too, the shells of dead crabs, penknives, model aircraft, books . . . and so on, and on, and on.

And when Jimmy Zest started collecting something, he went mad for it. He was at his worst one week in April just after he'd finished making a brand new money-box. To get money to put in it, he tortured his relatives and friends to give him jobs, charged young children fifty pence to see his puppet show and collected up money-back bottles. He would have gone so far as to play the mouth-organ in the street, cap in hand, if his mother had allowed him. He even thought up a scheme to get money out of his friends at school.

It began one Friday morning when Miss Quick left the classroom to go for her cup of coffee. She was no sooner out of the door than up went the lid of Jimmy Zest's desk, where he had stored a heap of stuff. He had a packet of wine gums in there, a bag of balloons and a box of crackers left over from Christmas. He'd found them in the attic, in the battered old container where the Christmas decorations were kept.

Jimmy Zest called to the rest of the class, "Roll up, roll up. Get your April crackers here. April crackers on sale now, roll up!"

Penny Brown, Gowso, Knuckles, Shorty and the others were anxious to get out to play: but they had never heard of April crackers before. So they paused and looked at each other and wondered what Jimmy Zest was up to.

Gowso was one of the first to come over for a closer look. Shorty came too, and Knuckles, who elbowed his way to the front for a good view. Mandy Taylor was careful not to stand too close to Knuckles. Legweak was right at the back when Jimmy Zest held up a yellow cracker for them all to see. "Get your April crackers here. Only one dozen left now, one dozen only."

"How much?" asked Gowso.

"Twenty pence."

"Your head's a marble, Zesty," Legweak pointed out, and another voice declared that they were no different from ordinary crackers.

The undismayed Jimmy Zest ignored the last speaker, who happened to be Penny Brown.

"Was it made in Hong Kong?" shouted Knuckles.

"They could be Hong Kong crackers," said Jimmy Zest, nodding his head. "With every April cracker you get a free balloon. That's a guarantee."

This news made Shorty twist round to see what somebody else thought of such generosity.

"*And* a free wine gum," said Jimmy Zest. "For just twenty pence you get a free balloon, a wine gum, and an April cracker."

Mandy Taylor said out loud, "You know, that's really good value," and the others believed her, for it was well known that Mandy Taylor did all the shopping in her house.

The April crackers began to sell. Gowso bought one, and Mandy, and when Shorty reached into his pocket for money, Knuckles went one better and bought two. Legweak called out in desperation, "Can I bring you my money after dinner, Zesty?"

Jimmy Zest took a note of his name and address.

Shorty Alexander and Jimmy Zest were walking down the hill after school when Penny

Brown caught up with them. She enjoyed walking home with either one of these two. Shorty was always doing interesting things like kicking his schoolbag to death or making up rules never to walk on the cracks in the pavement. Zesty was different. He walked home with his schoolbag on his back and never *did* anything. What he *said* was often very interesting, though.

"How much money did you get for your April crackers, Zesty?" Penny asked.

"If you'd bought one I'd tell you, Penelope," came the reply.

"Huh. All I did was ask."

"I got one hundred and sixty pence."

This brought a little nod from Shorty, who was a great admirer of Jimmy Zest's.

"Is it for a good cause or something?" Penny asked.

"Yes. It's for my giant money-box. I've got a money-box eight metres long."

Penny Brown, always on the look-out for his tricks, said, "Zesty!"

Shorty was more trusting. "An eight metre, giant money-box! You're definitely a genius, Zesty."

Suddenly, Penny Brown stopped dead with her back to a lamp-post. She took eight giant steps, and turned, and folded her arms.

"You must think we're stupid. Well we're not, are we, Shorty?"

"I am a bit," Shorty confessed frankly.

"Well *I'm* not stupid. A money-box from over there to over here! I get fed up with you sometimes."

Jimmy Zest stood with his hands up his blazer sleeves, like a Chinaman. "You didn't take big enough steps, Penelope. My money-box is longer than that."

Just for the moment, Penny Brown wasn't quite sure what to say. Jimmy Zest had created some great things in his lifetime, including the egg-box dinosaur which had stood in the corner of the school canteen for a week. But an eight-metre money-box . . . ? "Show us it, then!"

Ten minutes later the three of them stood on Jimmy Zest's doorstep. His mother said yes, they could come in if they took off their dirty feet. "She means your shoes," Jimmy Zest explained.

In they went. The money-box was a knobbly looking thing tucked into a corner at the foot of the stairs. Obviously it had been made from a mixture of cereal packets and egg boxes. A tube came out of the top of the box, and this tube ran up the stairs like a second bannister rail.

"Kitchen-roll tubes," explained Jimmy Zest as he led the other two up the stairs. "Here, where the tube goes round the bend, it's not quite so good. Fifty-pence pieces get stuck on the way down."

At the top of the stairs the tube of joined kitchen rolls ran up the wall and into the bedroom. And now, the maker of this marvellous thing took a handful of coins from his pocket and stood on a stool. "Listen," he said.

In dropped the coins. They rattled all the way down and bedded into the other coins at the bottom of the tube with a quiet tinkle.

"Nearly eight metres, I've measured it. Have a go, Penelope."

"Give me a coin."

"I haven't any more."

Penny Brown fished out a two-pound coin, the one she was going to use for Mandy's birthday present. In went the coin, down the tube, round the bend right to the bottom.

"You're a genius, Zesty," Shorty said again. "It's like a helter-skelter for your loose change. Who'd have thought of a giant money-box?"

"Come on," said Penny, "let's go down and get my two-pound coin."

Up went Jimmy Zest's hand. A very serious expression came over his face. "Can't be done, Penelope." He sounded very sorry. "You can't muck about with a money-box like this one – this is the only way in."

Penny Brown was not the sort to kick up a fuss in somebody else's house. On the other hand she didn't take too kindly to losing serious money. So she whispered furiously, "What about my two-pound coin?"

"You can have it back."

"When?"

"When I open the box."

"When's that?"

"When it's full."

"Zesty!"

"In about six months. You can see it's a very big money-box, Penelope. I'm doing my best to save."

Penny Brown struggled for the words to say what she was thinking. "But . . . six months! April-May-June . . . September! After the holidays. And what about Mandy's present?"

The sorrowful Jimmy Zest shrugged his shoulders in a hard-luck sort of way.

"You are money-mad, Jimmy Zest. You're a miser. You build great things like this just to *cheat* people, you're low, low, low, and you get up my nose!"

The lowly Jimmy Zest accepted this criticism calmly and offered Penny more April crackers out of a fresh box, but by this time they were out in the garden and it was war.

"No! You'll be sorry, you miser. You'll not get away with stealing other people's money."

"I'm only keeping it for six months, Penelope."

"*Kidnapping* people's money, then. Are you coming, Shorty?"

Shorty didn't know what to do, now that he was forced to take sides. True, he admired Jimmy Zest; but on the other hand he was keen on Penny Brown, who was now storming down the road like a horse that had never heard of reins.

Shorty wandered off towards the shops, vowing to come home from school with his brother the next day.

In fact Shorty did not have to go to school the next day, for it was a Saturday. Even so, the news of Jimmy Zest's eight-metre money-box spread rapidly among those who knew him. Gowso heard about it from Shorty while they were waiting to buy chips, and he told Legweak. And so, on Sunday afternoon, Legweak and Gowso went calling on Jimmy Zest to see the famous article for themselves.

As it happened, however, the Zest family was away for the day. Legweak had the good sense to poke open the letter-box of the front door to see what they could see.

They saw a blue carpet on the hall floor, a telephone-table-cum-seat, and a long, thin mirror. Gowso, when he finally laid eyes on the money-box tucked away at the foot of the stairs, said it reminded him of a Norman castle with a stretched chimney. Legweak said it was a very good idea to build a giant money-box, but really, he thought he could do just as well himself with a little time and effort.

Both boys went home to plan their money-boxes.

Monday morning did not start well for Jimmy Zest. No sooner was he through the door of the classroom than he found Mandy Taylor and Penny Brown waiting for him – with a complaint.

First Penny Brown warned him that the girls in the class had agreed not to speak to him until he'd given back the two-pound coin he'd kidnapped. Then Mandy Taylor waved a balloon under his nose and complained that the free balloon she'd got with her April cracker had a hole in it.

"That hole is supposed to be there, Amanda," Jimmy Zest explained. "It's the hole you blow through to make the balloon go up."

"Not *that* hole," snapped Mandy, "the balloon goes down when you blow it up."

"Then you mean it has *two* holes."

Jimmy Zest nodded his head as if this was indeed a disgrace.

"You're entitled to your money back, Amanda. Let me have everything back and you'll get a refund. Have you got your April cracker?"

After poking about in her schoolbag, Mandy produced one half of her exploded cracker.

"That's OK, Amanda," said the reasonable Jimmy Zest, "now your wine gum."

"I ate my wine gum."

"I'll accept it even if it's chewed up."

"I *swallowed* my wine gum."

"Sorry, no refund," said Jimmy Zest as Miss Quick came into the room to start lessons.

And that was that. Penny Brown and Mandy Taylor nodded grimly to one another as if they meant business, and Mandy immediately swopped seats with Legweak to get away from the despicable Jimmy Zest. This meant that she had to sit beside Knuckles, who frightened her to death, but it was worth it. Knuckles was just plain bad, he was not a miser or a cheat.

There was something different about Legweak this Monday morning. He had a giant brown paper parcel which he carried about with him. It was sitting by the side of his desk. Every now and then, when Miss Quick's back was turned, he hissed at Jimmy Zest and pointed down at the parcel and tried to whisper a message.

Miss Quick caught him at it. "Stephen Armstrong," – Armstrong was Legweak's real name – "what are you whispering about? And what have you got in that parcel that's so important?"

Legweak looked at her as if to say "I thought you'd never ask" and began to peel off the paper. Slowly, a most peculiar sight came into view. It was a dirty grey colour, and written over, so it

seemed, by a thousand biros. Proudly, Legweak set it up on the desk for the truth to strike everybody.

"It's some kind of leg."

"Never."

"It *is* a leg."

"Then it's false."

"It's a plaster of Paris leg."

Legweak nodded at Mandy Taylor, who had guessed correctly.

"It was my cousin's, he had an accident playing football. Miss, he had two thousand signatures on that plaster. You can count them if you don't believe me."

There was suddenly a lot of wild speculation

about the false leg – until CLAP! went Miss Quick's hands, and back to their seats went those who had come creeping for a closer look. Then Miss Quick asked: "Stephen, *why* did you bring your cousin's plaster leg to school with you?"

"To show Philip and Zesty, Miss. It's a money-box, see? I stuck up the sides and closed over the top. The money goes in that hole."

"I see. Very good, Stephen. Now put it away like a good boy and show it to your friends at lunch-time."

Legweak was as pleased as Punch at the success of his plaster money-box, especially when Jimmy Zest leaned over and congratulated him on a very fine effort indeed.

Penny Brown sat seething with anger all through the afternoon. Jimmy Zest never looked near her once, he sat doing algebra and getting his sums right while the rest of the class struggled with arithmetic, and all the while her two-pound coin was lying at the bottom of his silly big money-box. It made her boil!

Which is why she and Mandy Taylor tackled him when they saw him and Gowso sitting on the school gates at the end of the school day.

"Right! Where's my money, Zesty?" Penny, with her feet planted wide apart and her hands on her hips, was the very picture of determination. Gowso was on Zesty's side and spoiling for a fight with the two girls, but Jimmy Zest's head nodded in sympathy with Penny Brown as he took a crumpled piece of paper out of his pocket.

"I thought about it over the weekend, Penelope," he said sadly. "I don't feel good about having your money. Here."

> I, JIMMY ZEST, owe PENELOPE
> BROWN the sum of two pounds
> sterling when my money-box is
> opened.

Penny stared at the message, then at the person who had printed it.

"This is no good to me. I want my money *now*. And so does Mandy. She wants her birthday present."

"I can't destroy my money-box."

"You're in big trouble, Jimmy Zest," Mandy Taylor joined in. "You're robbing two people, her and me. The police are just down the road, you know."

"I don't think they'd be bothered," said Jimmy Zest.

"Oh would they *not*? You dare come with us,

14

then, and we'll see."

Mandy Taylor took off down the school hill with Penny Brown after her, running. They were followed after a short interval by Jimmy Zest and Gowso, who confidently declared that the girls were bluffing. After a quick march for five minutes, the four of them stood at the steps below the big heavy door of the police station.

"We're here," said Jimmy Zest.

"Go on, Penny," Mandy Taylor said indignantly, "you're in the right. Show him!"

Penny Brown looked rather doubtfully at the door of the police station. This was an awful mess that Mandy had got her into. She turned to Jimmy Zest to give him a last chance. Then, because she fancied that she saw a smile on that face, she ran up the steps and went right in.

Gowso began to fidget. "Come on, Zesty, time to go home." Pause. "*Home* time, Zesty, I said I wouldn't be late." Pause. "Will you come on?" And now, as the door of the police station began to open, "See you, Zesty."

Away went Gowso at the run just as Penny Brown appeared in the company of a tall police sergeant.

"*Now* you're for it," whispered Mandy Taylor, giving the ring on her finger a nervous twist.

Jimmy Zest waited as they came down the steps towards him, the policeman with his big black boots creaking. Shiny big boots. Penny Brown had her hands behind her back and was looking straight at the ground as the policeman pointed towards the town.

"It's not too easy if you don't know the town, love," the sergeant was saying, "but you go to the second set of traffic lights and turn left and that'll take you right to the place. It's a long road, mind."

"Thank you, sir."

"Have a good time, now."

"Yes, sir."

When the policeman went in again, Penny Brown spun on her heel to say vile things to Jimmy Zest, who had heard it all: but he was already on his way home, jogging.

"I couldn't say it," Penny confessed to Mandy, "my legs went to jelly when I got to the counter. Just you wait, Jimmy Zest," she called out to the diminishing figure in the distance, "I'll get you!"

Unable to bring the full weight of the law down on the head of James Zest, Penny had asked the way to the museum, instead.

That evening after tea, when Penny Brown was out for a spin on her bike, she met Knuckles and Shorty near the shops. They were carrying a hefty

16

log between them. When they saw Penny they set the log down and seemed glad of the rest.

"Where did you get it?" she asked them.

"It's a branch," said Shorty, "it fell off a tree."

Penny looked hard at the hatchet tucked into Knuckles's belt. Probably this was the trunk of a beautiful cherry tree from somebody's front garden. However, Penny had a problem of her own to talk about. She said it was a crime and a shame that somebody could kidnap your money from April to September.

"It won't be worth two pounds by then, Shorty. Inflation will have got to it and eaten it away."

Shorty shook his head wisely. "Inflation?" He didn't like the sound of it. "What's inflation?"

"A disease that affects money. Mandy thinks I should go to the police."

Knuckles, whose grandfather had been a cat burglar before the war, said that Mandy Taylor needed her head seen to. He and Shorty picked up their log and went marching home.

Two more giant money-boxes made their first appearances in public the next morning. One belonged to Brian Parks, and his effort was much admired. His idea had been to turn an old television cabinet into a money-box by blocking up the screen hole with plywood. Then all it needed was a slit in the top to take the money.

The other effort was Gowso's. He brought in a wire budgie cage plastered with papier mâché and with a funnel coming out of the top instead of a slot. Legweak said that it might be rather easy to break into a thing made out of *papier mâché*. Gowso, who was not very good at taking criticism, snarled that it was a money-box and not a bank, and anyway, what was to stop you sticking a plaster of Paris leg under your arm and running away with it, money-box and all?

Later in the morning, when Miss Quick had the class nicely settled and the smell of school dinners was in the air, there was a very loud BANG! The teacher jumped about two feet in the air and whipped round from the blackboard to stare at the class with murder in her eyes. Knuckles had an innocent big grin all over his face. Beside him, crying her eyes out, was Mandy Taylor.

Four gigantic strides took Miss Quick down the aisle between the desks to the scene of the crime.

"Wha . . . wha . . . wha . . ." Mandy Taylor said as she breathed in with great heaving sobs.

Miss Quick ignored her and stood hovering over Knuckles like a cloud about to burst.

"What did you do?"

"Nothing, Miss."

"You did not do nothing."

"I didn't, Miss."

The remains of the grin were still there, for teachers did not easily frighten Knuckles. Miss Quick surrounded him with nice people like Mandy and Penny in the hope that they would keep him out of trouble and encourage him to do his work instead of talking about football and bonfires. "Nicholas Alexander, what did you *do* to her!"

From under his desk, Knuckles produced half of an exploded cracker.

"We only pulled an April cracker, Miss."

"He made me, he *made* me," Mandy wailed, "he said he'd put blots all over my page if I didn't pull the Hong Kong cracker with him."

Miss Quick nodded grimly, and knew that she'd heard the truth.

"I'll put blots all over *him*," she muttered. "Mandy, stop that crying for goodness' sake." She turned to Knuckles. "What kind of cracker did you say?"

"An April cracker, Miss, made in Hong Kong."

The teacher took the remains of the cracker and examined it.

"Now you're trying to be funny. This is an ordinary Christmas cracker."

"No, Miss, that's an April cracker, I bought two from Zesty. He sells them cheap."

Penny Brown threw a wicked glance at Jimmy Zest, as if to say, "Now see what trouble you've got people into", then turned back to listen to Miss Quick warning Knuckles that if he let off any more Christmas crackers in April or any other month he would go home on crutches.

"And what's more," said Miss Quick, addressing the whole class and pointing at the *papier mâché* budgie cage, "no more money-boxes are to come into this classroom. I've seen three and three is plenty. Keep that sort of thing for your craft teacher. And now – take down your homework!"

The homework was a stinker – three whole pages of a story about a day on the beach. Penny Brown looked hard at Jimmy Zest to see if he felt guilty at everything that had happened, for every bit of it was his fault. But he didn't seem to be in the least concerned.

If Miss Quick thought she had seen the last of the giant money-boxes, she was mistaken. There was one more to come – the creation of the Alexander twins.

She was walking round the playground at lunchtime, keeping an eye on things, when she saw Noel Alexander standing beside one of the long drainpipes that ran from the roof of the school to the ground.

The boy had a cardboard box in his hand. Gathered round him was a small gallery of interested spectators. As Miss Quick came closer she saw that it was an empty potato-crisp box, and the boy had somehow fitted it over the mouth of the long pipe.

"Noel Alexander, what are you doing with that drainpipe?"

Shorty turned and saw Miss Quick and knew he was done for. But he did his best. "I'm just standing here, Miss."

"Why are you holding that carton under that drainpipe? What are you expecting to come down it? Gold?"

It was not a bad guess. The quiet, tinkling sound of something falling down the inside of the long pipe reached her ears. Miss Quick peered into the box and saw two coins, a one pence and a two pence. From some distance away, and from a great height, a voice began to call.

"What about that one, Shorteee? Did she come down?"

Shorty flashed a sick sort of grin at Miss Quick, who was rapidly putting one and one together and getting two. If Shorty Alexander was down here, then up there, on the roof, must be . . .

"Come down!" she screamed at the figure who was suddenly trying to hide on the flat roof, "Nicholas Alexander, what are you doing up there?"

A red head appeared over the rim of the roof. "He's going to be a fireman when he grows up, Miss," Shorty said, as if that might make some difference.

"If he ever grows up," snapped Miss Quick. "Do you hear me up there? Come down this instant!"

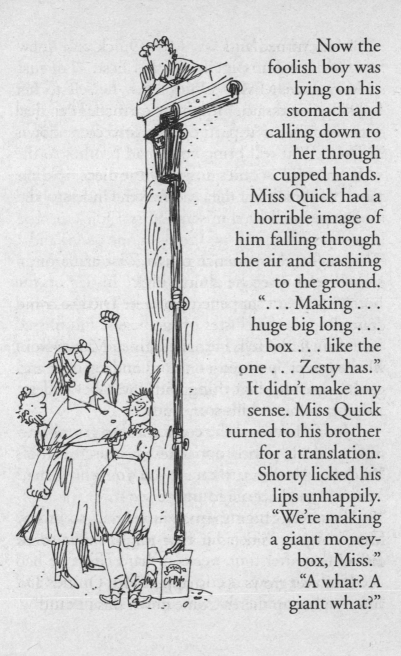

Now the foolish boy was lying on his stomach and calling down to her through cupped hands. Miss Quick had a horrible image of him falling through the air and crashing to the ground. "... Making ... huge big long ... box ... like the one ... Zesty has." It didn't make any sense. Miss Quick turned to his brother for a translation. Shorty licked his lips unhappily. "We're making a giant money-box, Miss." "A what? A giant what?"

"Money-box, Miss."

"Out of a drainpipe?"

Very gravely, Miss Quick drew herself to her full height and said, "You boys are mad. I can deal with badness, it's part of my job. But this is different. You will bring your mad brother to the staff-room if he comes down in one piece, and the three of us shall visit the headmaster. Understood?"

Shorty swallowed miserably.

That night, the patience of Mr Zest came to an sudden end when he almost broke his leg on the bottom stair. It happened when he tried to avoid trampling on the cluster of egg boxes, and missed his footing, and fell. He called his son down from his bedroom, pointed at the offending box, and said, "Open up that thing with the tubes and get rid of it before it kills somebody."

Mrs Zest entered the conversation, grumbling. "I can't shut his bedroom door because of it. It's become a tourist attraction, did you know that? People actually come round to see it."

They were ganging up on him again, so Jimmy Zest obliged. When he counted his money, he found that after four weeks of hard effort he had accumulated the pathetic sum of four pounds and forty-eight pence. It was most disappointing, particularly since two pounds of it belonged to somebody else.

Five minutes later, Penny Brown was called down from her bedroom, where she was reading about bees in an encyclopedia.

"Phone for you, Penny," her father said.

It wasn't Mandy, as she'd thought.

"I was thinking about you, Penelope," she heard him say, "about you and your two-pound coin."

"Oh?" Penny said cautiously. This might well be another crooked fiddle.

"It's time you had your money back, Penelope. Six months is too long a time for you to wait. When is Amanda's birthday?"

"Saturday."

"I'll bring it into school tomorrow. Will that give you time to get her a present?"

"Actually I was just going to get her a packet of felt tips."

"Oh, very useful, Penelope."

This was unexpectedly decent behaviour from Jimmy Zest. Imagine him thinking about her like that.

Jimmy Zest had some very good points, after all. Penny had actually heard him congratulating Knuckles and Shorty on their stupid drainpipe money-box idea – he wasn't a bit jealous of people.

Really, she liked Jimmy Zest quite a lot.

"Are you still there, Penelope?"

"Yes. See you tomorrow with my money, Zesty, OK?"

- 2 -

A Death in the Park

Mandy Taylor caused a sensation on Wednesday afternoon. She brought a dog into school.

Shorty and Legweak and Gowso saw her leading it down the corridor and they thought they were dreaming, for it was bigger than a sheep. "Jeepers creepers," said Gowso.

That wasn't all. Mandy Taylor walked the dog right into the classroom and made it lie down at her feet.

"Miss," Gowso said in tones of wonder. "Look at that!"

"I see it, Philip," said Miss Quick. "It's only a dog. Mandy has my permission to bring it in for the debate this afternoon. I believe it belongs to your neighbours, Mandy, isn't that right? Tell us his name."

"He's called Walter, Miss Quick. He's an Old English Sheepdog, that's why he's so hairy."

Miss Quick tapped her desk with a pencil to

hurry the late people.

"Seats, please, everyone – we are about to begin the debate. Stephen, you will speak first."

A hush fell over the room, for the pupils of Miss Quick's class loved the excitement of a debate. This Wednesday afternoon the subject was "Dogs do not make suitable pets" and the main speakers were Stephen Armstrong – that is, Legweak – and Penny Brown.

Legweak was against dogs. He said they were only a nuisance, they pulled rubbish out of bins and fouled up the pavements and also they were walking flea-pits. He gave dogs such awful abuse that Shorty couldn't take it.

"Miss," he shouted, "my aunty in the country has a dog. It kills rats and they're the enemies of the human race."

"Here, here," said Penny Brown.

Miss Quick's pencil rattled on the desk. She did not like interruptions.

"Noel, this is a debate. Wait until it's your turn to speak."

It was Penny's turn now to rise to her feet and point out how useful dogs were – she mentioned police dogs and huskies and guide dogs for the blind.

Then Jimmy Zest got up with a speech three

pages long in his hand. One day, thought Penny Brown, the world would run out of paper and the reason would be Jimmy Zest.

He was against dogs, which was a pity. It was very
difficult to win a debate against Jimmy Zest because his arguments were usually so good. He didn't actually say that dogs should be banned, but he said that the licence fee ought to be raised to five hundred pounds. The snook had brought in two newspaper cuttings – one about dogs worrying sheep and the other about an Alsatian which had attacked a baby in a pram.

Slowly, Mandy Taylor rose to her feet to cut Jimmy Zest down to size.

"Listen, everybody, Jimmy Zest is just trying to scare you. Dogs love people and people love dogs. Just like Walter. Miss, would you like to see Walter doing tricks?"

Jimmy Zest and Legweak objected at once, they said it wasn't fair. But Miss Quick overruled them, and a short interval occurred while Walter sat up

and begged, rolled over dead, and shook hands with Mandy Taylor, who said: "There you are, Legweak, anybody can see that dogs are not a nuisance. And dogs don't eat babies, Jimmy Zest, and nobody's going to vote for you!"

Mandy Taylor was almost right. When Miss Quick counted hands, only one person voted with Jimmy Zest, and that was Legweak.

It was a resounding victory for the doggy people. Shorty crossed the room to shake Walter by the paw and Miss Quick said that by the look of things, dogs were here to stay.

After school, the defeated Jimmy Zest walked down the school hill in the company of Penny Brown, Shorty, Mandy Taylor and Walter, who plodded along patiently at the end of his lead like an overgrown mop. At the bottom of the hill they turned left into the park. This was the long way home, but Mandy thought that Walter would probably enjoy it better if he was away from smoky lorries and things.

"You should let Walter off that lead, you're choking him," Shorty said.

"I can't, Shorty," Mandy replied. "He's not my dog. I only borrowed him for the afternoon and he's my responsibility.

"I thought you said he was well trained,"

observed Jimmy Zest. "If he's well trained, he'll come back when you call him."

Of course Penny Brown saw immediately what he was driving at – he was trying to imply that Walter was unsafe, like some jungle tiger. So the girls had a quick discussion, and decided to let Walter off his lead. There was no traffic in the park, after all, and anyway, Walter was such a big lamb that he wouldn't bite anybody. Mandy buried her hand in Walter's woolly neck to unclip his lead.

It made no difference. Walter sat with his pink tongue flopping in his beardy face, and watched the world go by.

"See, Zesty?" said Penny Brown.

Unfortunately, that was the moment when Walter spotted something interesting waddling along the avenue in the park – a fat little Jack Russell terrier. He bounded over in his lollopy way to make friends.

When that terrier saw Walter coming, he stiffened, and strained so hard that his owner could hardly hold him on the lead. The savage little brute flew into a rage and stood up on his hind legs to get at Walter, and made such an angry racket that poor Walter disappeared at top speed down the tree-lined avenue.

Mandy Taylor took a few steps after him. "Walter, come back. WALTER, YOU BAD DOG!"

The situation grew worse. The owner of the Jack Russell terrier came over to roar at them. "Why don't you keep that animal under control?"

He was an old man in a flat cap. Mandy blushed until her feet felt warm and Penny said: "Our dog was only sniffing yours."

"Can you not read? There's a sign back there says you have to keep your dog on a lead. Any more cheek and I'll report you."

When he was well away from them, Penny Brown said: "People like that get up my nose."

Meanwhile, Mandy was panicking.

"Please, Shorty, whistle for him. I told you we shouldn't have let him off the lead, he's only borrowed."

Big Walter was gone for about ten minutes. Jimmy Zest used the time to tell the others a true horror story which he had forgotten to use in the debate. A collie dog got excited and bit off a piece of its owner's ear, so they rushed him to the hospital and brought the bit of ear with them and the doctors stitched it on again.

"Micro-surgery, they call it," Jimmy Zest explained, just as Walter came bounding towards them from the high side of the park.

Walter lolloped along, as usual, but he carried his head rather close to the ground.

"He's got something in his mouth," Jimmy Zest said.

"Somebody's ear," suggested Shorty.

That dog had a hen in his mouth. A whole hen. "Oh flute!" said Penny Brown.

Mandy Taylor could not speak at all. She reached out and squeezed Penny's arm until her knuckles turned white. And Walter, while everybody stared at him, stood quite still with his tail wagging and his mouth full. No dog had ever looked more pleased with himself.

Shorty took Walter by the chin and shook his jaw.

"Walter, let go. There's a good boy, let go."

"WALTER WILL YOU LET GO THIS MINUTE!" yelled Mandy Taylor – and the hen plopped out of Walter's mouth into Shorty's hand.

Not a feather twitched. That hen didn't even move when Shorty gave it a prod. After tapping it on the beak and making the head flop from side to side, he was satisfied.

"Dead as a doornail," he pronounced.

Mandy Taylor simply couldn't face the hen's beady black eyes. Her heart was thumping like a

drum as she thought about what people would say. And anyway, how could a dog that wouldn't say boo to a goose suddenly turn round and kill a hen? A harmless hen?

At last she could speak.

"Penny, what are we going to do? We shouldn't have let it off the lead. That was your fault, Jimmy Zest. I blame *you*."

"You needn't bother," said Jimmy Zest. "I had nothing to do with it."

They argued helplessly for a minute or so until Penny saw the man in the flat cap returning with his rotten dog.

"Look, Mandy, we don't have to tell anybody

about this. Put Walter's lead on and we'll take him back as if it hasn't happened."

"But what about that . . . hen?"

"We'll bury it. Who's going to worry about a chicken? Shorty, stick it up your jumper and come on."

Shorty did as he was told and tucked the hen under his armpit so that none of it showed. They scraped a hole in a soft bank of leaf mould on the high side of the park and Penny made Shorty and Zesty promise not to breathe a word about this happening to any living soul – especially not to Gowso, who was known to be a gossip.

In this way they got rid of the evidence. Mandy Taylor felt a little better now that their crime had been concealed under a mound of twigs. But Walter knew. He jumped about cheerfully at the end of his lead without the least idea that the authorities could be after him, not to mention the hen's angry owner.

On the way to school the following day, Penny Brown and Mandy Taylor met Gowso and Legweak.

Legweak began to bark like a dog, and chased after Gowso, who clucked like a frightened hen.

"Bow wow!"

"Bwaak cluck-cluck!"

"Bow-wow-wow."

Gowso flapped his elbows and stuck out his neck. "Bwak buk buk. Help. A big dog called Walter is after me and I'm only a poor hen. Bwak buk buk bwaaak!"

"Shut up, Gowso you zombie," called Penny Brown, "or I'll pull your plug out!"

"But how did they find out?" cried Mandy.

There was no mystery about that. The news that Mandy Taylor had been in charge of a dog which had killed a chicken in the park – that kind of secret was bound to get out. As a matter of fact, it had remained a secret for less than an hour, for Shorty had told Legweak in exchange for a bit of his pickled boiled egg.

On this Thursday morning, Mandy and Penny chose to ignore the antics of twits like Gowso and Legweak. Then Gowso said something which could not be ignored.

"It'll have to be put down, you know."

Mandy Taylor stopped dead in her tracks and spun round.

"What do you mean 'put down', Gowso?"

"Executed," said Gowso, and pulled a finger across his throat. "It's got the taste of blood, you see. It'll kill again."

"Don't listen to him, Mandy," warned Penny Brown. This was just another piece of typical Gowso chat. If there was a way to be pessimistic, he would find it. "He doesn't know what he's talking about."

All the same, Mandy looked quite worried as she climbed the school hill. It was bad enough that some people now knew about the dead hen, but this latest development was a hundred times worse. Walter could be executed for it! Could Gowso be right? Big Walter was a dog who went to shows and won prizes and now, possibly . . . Mandy twisted nervously at the ring on her little finger. Now, possibly, Walter was – doomed.

That afternoon, Penny Brown made a point of walking home with Jimmy Zest so that she could find out what he thought about Walter and the hen. Of all people in this time of crisis he was the one most likely to talk sense, unlike Gowso or Legweak who said the first daft thing that came into their heads.

Jimmy Zest knew a lot about how the world worked. He was the cleverest person in the class – cleverer, even, than Mandy – and he didn't get into awful trouble like Knuckles and Shorty, or not very often, anyway. Also, he was very good at making things. In fact, Penny Brown was thinking as she came down the school hill with him, he was a very good example of the kind of person you would want on your desert island if you were shipwrecked.

"Zesty," she said, "Legweak told Mandy they'll cut Walter's head off. But they don't do that sort of thing nowadays, do they?"

"No. They'll fix electric wires to the dog's hind legs, also its ears, and electrocute it."

Flute! Poor big Walter. It was a good job Mandy wasn't present to hear *that*.

"Zesty, I think she'll have to tell, don't you? I said I would go with her to see Walter's owners. What do you think?"

"I'll show you something," said Jimmy Zest.

At the bottom of the hill he turned left into the park. He kept to the high path under the beech trees, and beyond the beeches a spindly laurel hedge marked the boundary between the park and the gardens of the houses beyond.

Jimmy Zest bent double to peer through.

"What are you looking for, Zesty?"

"Hens."

In one of the gardens Penny noticed a long cage with half a dozen banties strutting about inside the wire netting. They seemed nervous – those hens hardly took time to peck. It was as if they expected Walter to come among them at any moment.

"I'd hate to be a hen," said Penny Brown, just as a man came out of the house wearing a plastic coat and cap.

Penny recognized him at once.

"Oh no! It's Mr Jones's house."

"The patrolman," said Jimmy Zest. "It's his hen. I should have realized it before. I only remembered at break time."

"You never knew he had hens, Zesty."

"I did. He sells eggs to the cleaning ladies."

Mr Jones was the person who stopped the traffic with his big lollipop, and Penny Brown could not fail to see how this made the whole bad business even worse. As well as trouble at home, Mandy would have to face Mr Jones in school.

Meanwhile, Jimmy Zest used the side of his foot to scoop the body of the famous hen from its mouldy hole in the ground. He lifted the thing up by its spiky feet and said: "Got it. Let's go."

"Where are you taking that hen, Zesty?"

"I've got an idea. I'm taking it home."

Not with *her*, he wasn't,

"Are you wise, Jimmy Zest!"

What would people think if they saw that creature with its gawky head trailing along the public street? Almost certainly it was crawling with nits and lice, and just waiting to set up house on the nearest living thing.

"Sometimes, Zesty," she told him, "I wonder if you're even human."

Jimmy Zest did not go into his house when he arrived home from school that day. Instead, he took the hen into the garage and closed the door so that he could be alone. Then he spread newspapers on the floor and began to pluck the hen, feather by feather, until it resembled the kind of chicken you buy at the supermarket.

And now he inspected it closely for damage.

Suddenly the garage door opened. In came a whirl of wind – and whoosh! the pile of feathers scattered high up and low down, and some of them settled like snow on the head and shoulders of the startled Jimmy Zest.

It was his mother. She had a shovel in her hand as she came to fetch some coal. She stopped when she saw her son decorated with dirty-white plumes and with a pink, plucked chicken in his hand.

Very slowly, she pronounced each word.

"What – are – you – doing?"

"It's a hen."

"That is no answer, I can see it's a hen."

"I'm doing a post-mortem."

"On a hen? You're doing a post-mortem on a *hen?*"

"A dog killed it, you see," said Jimmy Zest. "I'm looking for teeth marks but I don't see any."

His mother glared at the hen's pimply body. Then she pointed at the feathers with her shovel.

"It probably died of a heart attack. Get that mess cleaned up. And wash those hands in disinfectant. Honestly, I wonder are you getting more sense or less?"

While Jimmy Zest conducted his forensic examination of the dead chicken, Penny and

Mandy walked down to the greengrocer's to do a message.

They were thinking that life could be very cruel sometimes.

"That's what he said, Mandy. Electric wires on its back legs and ears. Its *ears*."

"If we'd even done something *bad*," said Mandy in anguish. "It's always the good people who suffer if you ask me. I'll never look Mr Jones in the face again, suppose he finds out?"

As they came out of the greengrocer's Penny Brown said, "At least things can't get any worse," but she was wrong. Nicholas Alexander saw them and screeched to a halt on his bike.

"Vroom, vroom, VROOM," he said. "Give me an apple."

"No," said Penny Brown. "We will not give you an apple. Buy your own apples if you want apples."

"I'm broke," said Knuckles. "Vroom vroom."

No doubt this was him ticking over on his pretend motorbike. Actually, he was riding Legweak's bicycle, for Nicholas Alexander never used his own equipment, always somebody else's. He borrowed Mandy's colouring pencils all the time because she was afraid to say "No" to him. Then he sharpened them away to nothing. In no time at all he could turn a lovely tall pencil into a dwarf.

"Vroom," said Knuckles, "give me an apple or I'll tell the patrolman your dog killed his hen."

He knew! Mandy almost dropped her bag of groceries. Penny said: "That is blackmail, Nicholas Alexander."

"Killing chickens – that's murder. Give me an apple."

Immediately, Mandy threw him an apple and he rode away delighted with himself.

"Like a grizzly bear at the zoo!" Penny shouted after him. She thought that Mandy had just done something very stupid indeed. "Tomorrow he'll come back for another apple, and another apple. He'll want more than apples, Mandy."

"You don't seem to understand something, Penny," said Mandy, "Walter's life is at stake."

And she became quite tearful as they walked up the road.

Fractions.

That's how Friday started in school. Everybody was quiet as Miss Quick explained that one over two was just the same as four over eight or eight over sixteen. After talking at the board for a little while, Miss Quick paused to ask a question.

"How many sixteenths could you divide a whole cake into? Hands only, please."

The first hand up belonged to Shorty, which astonished all who saw it. It was common knowledge that he couldn't tell the difference between a vulgar fraction and a decimal point.

"Miss. If your dog kills a chicken in the park, does it have to be executed?"

The look on Miss Quick's face suggested that she would like to execute Shorty.

Gowso spoke up.

"My dad says, Miss, if it's got the taste of blood it's dangerous."

Miss Quick, who had breathed in deeply in order to let loose a shout at somebody, allowed her used air to escape slowly.

"A dog which kills livestock," she said patiently, "is always a risk. The proper word, Noel, is not 'executed' – such a dog is 'destroyed'. But the debate on dogs was yesterday, it is over."

Not yet, it wasn't. "Miss, Mandy Taylor's dog killed one of the patrolman's hens in the park on the way home from school," Gowso said.

"What!" said Miss Quick.

Penny Brown was on her feet and her face was flaming.

"Gowso, shut up! It wasn't even her dog, it lives

next door. People like you should be destroyed, Gowso, never mind dogs."

"Penny!"

"Sure it was only a hen, Miss," Shorty said helpfully. "Nobody would care about a hen."

"What about eggs?" shouted Legweak.

And then Mandy Taylor, who was normally very quiet in class and certainly one of Miss Quick's favourites, lost control.

"It was your fault, Shorty Alexander. If you hadn't told in the first place – but you wanted a bite of a pickled egg and now Walter's going to die, he's going to be destroyed." And with that, she sat down at her table – and cried.

The classroom was in uproar. Even Knuckles, who loved bustle and fuss, was a bit alarmed by the sudden letting loose of passions. Somehow, Miss Quick's carefully prepared lesson on fractions had turned into an emotional scene and she had to clap her hands and yell in order to restore the quiet and calm to which she was accustomed.

"That is quite enough, I have never seen the like of it. Nobody – absolutely nobody – will speak."

For a while, nobody did speak. Then Jimmy Zest stood up.

"Miss—"

"Sit down, James Zest. 'Nobody' includes you. Even you."

"But Miss, I spoke to the patrolman this morning."

All round the quiet room, ears were placed on red alert. Even Mandy raised her teary eyes suspiciously.

Miss Quick nodded. "Go on."

"Well, it *was* his hen, Miss. He had nine banties and now he's only got eight. He had a rooster at one time too, but the neighbours complained about it crowing and he had to get rid of it. He says some people don't like getting out of their beds in the morning."

"Get on with it, Jimmy Zest," said Miss Quick.

"Well, Miss, I examined the dead hen and I couldn't find any teeth marks you see. So I asked Mr Jones if one of his hens had died of natural causes – like maybe a heart attack – and if he had buried it in the park."

Miss Quick smiled a little. "Natural causes. And what did Mr Jones say to that?"

"Miss, he said yes."

The first person to realize the importance of all this was Penny Brown.

"Zesty. The hen was dead already – was it? Say it was dead already, Zesty."

"Miss, the hen was dead already. Walter just dug it up, that's all. It had an interesting smell."

Mandy Taylor rose slowly to her feet. Through her tears, her eyes were shining.

"Oh Zesty. You've saved Walter."

"Well . . . not really."

"Oh you have, Zesty, he'll not be destroyed. You've saved Walter."

Miss Quick allowed a few moments more for Mandy Taylor to beam with happiness and to express her gratitude to Jimmy Zest before resuming briskly.

"Right. Now that that is over, I think we'll pretend that it never happened. Let there be no more uproar in this classroom. I will go back to my earlier question, and try again. How many sixteenths could you divide a whole cake into — hands only, if you please."

Of course, Jimmy Zest's hand was up first, the way it always was. Watching him in action, Penny Brown couldn't help wondering how he always knew so much.

And yet it had been so obvious. Natural causes. Why hadn't she thought of those?

- 3 -

A Story with a Tail

Jimmy Zest made an interesting discovery the night his Uncle Henry called – he discovered that practically the whole world is insured.

It happened like this. Uncle Henry, after parking his motorbike at the side of the house, came into Jimmy Zest's hall wearing a heavy coat, thick gloves, and a yellow crash helmet. Uncle Henry gave his helmet a good hard tug to get it off – sometimes it stuck on his large ears – and the helmet smashed into the glass lampshade above his head.

The lampshade shattered into splinters. Jimmy Zest shut his eyes, and ducked. His mother let out a yell. Uncle Henry was horrified.

"I feel so stupid," he said.

No wonder, thought Jimmy Zest, for he had just done a very stupid thing. All you could see now was the bare electric light-bulb swinging at the end of the flex.

Jimmy Zest's mother sighed. "Henry, you are so clumsy."

"I know, I know. I'll buy you another one."

Uncle Henry took a step and crunched some glass into the carpet.

"Henry, don't bother. Just go into the living room and sit down like a mouse. Anyway, I dare say I can claim on insurance."

While Jimmy Zest helped his mother to clear up the mess in the hall they had a very interesting chat about insurance. He found out, for example, that his bike was insured so that if he lost it or had it stolen, the insurance company would pay out. Then his mum could buy him a new one.

"You can insure people, too," his mum said.

Jimmy Zest was amazed to hear that his dad's life was insured. If his dad died, his mum would receive a payment to help her with her money worries. This wasn't very nice to think about, but at least it showed that you could insure practically anything.

Their car was insured. So was their house. And the contents of their house. Even lampshades.

Then Jimmy Zest began to think how his friends Shorty and Gowso and Knuckles and Legweak were always losing stuff – insurance was exactly what they needed. Only last Monday,

Legweak had lost a chocolate-covered Waggon Wheel. Actually he claimed it had been stolen, but that didn't matter. If that Waggon Wheel had been insured, Legweak would have got another one. Absolutely free.

Thoughtfully, Jimmy Zest opened his jotter and wrote some figures on a clean page. He had had an interesting idea and he just wanted to add up a few sums to see if it would work.

In school next morning when Jimmy Zest announced that he was selling insurance, nobody paid any attention to him.

"WILL YOU LISTEN? I AM SELLING INSURANCE," he said again, determined to be heard over the racket that was going on in the classroom.

It was one of those wild days when the rotten weather kept everybody indoors during the morning break. Mandy Taylor and Penny Brown were busy playing a game of Hangman on the board with the teacher's chalk. Shorty Alexander was there too, offering hopeless advice, for his spelling was dreadful. Gowso sat on a desk with a long black case on his lap. This did not contain a machine gun, as Shorty sometimes claimed, but an ordinary violin. The school concert was coming up soon, so poor old Gowso had to carry this case with him wherever he went. He was refereeing an arm-wrestling contest between Knuckles and Legweak, who were stretched out on the floor.

In fact it was Knuckles Alexander who first lifted his head when Jimmy Zest mentioned insurance.

"Insurance? Did you say you're selling insurance, Zesty?"

"I did."

Knuckles got to his feet, covered in dust.

"We got a new carpet out of the insurance, Shorty burned a hole in our old one." He shouted across the room to Shorty, his twin brother: "Hey, Shorty, Zesty is selling insurance."

"Insure your pencils and rubbers very cheap. Also your break biscuits. I insure Kit Kats, sweets and Waggon Wheels plus apples, oranges and all fruit," said Jimmy Zest.

Legweak put up his left arm as if he was asking for permission to speak. His right arm had been wrecked by Knuckles in the arm-wrestling contest.

"I lost a Waggon Wheel last Monday."

"You should have been insured," said Jimmy Zest, "then you would have received compensation."

"What's that?" asked Shorty.

"Money for a new one," Penny Brown translated.

Penny and Mandy had left the blackboard and their game of Hangman to listen to Jimmy Zest. Penny Brown was not a bit impressed. She knew a little about insurance. She knew that you didn't get it for nothing.

"How much is it going to cost, Zesty?"

"Ten pence a week, Penelope."

"Huh."

"Who keeps the money?" Shorty wanted to know.

"*He* keeps the money," Mandy Taylor said into Shorty's face with great enthusiasm. "But he *pays* for things if we lose them, don't you see, Shorty? Suppose you lost something? Or broke it? Put me down for insurance, Zesty. I mean, what's ten pence nowadays?"

"Put me down too," shouted Legweak, no doubt with his Waggon Wheel in mind.

They all bought insurance, except for Penny Brown. Carefully, the methodical Jimmy Zest turned to the back page of his jotter, where he wrote down the names of his clients. He also made a list of the things which were insured: rulers, pencils and pens, all fruit, dinner tickets, all break

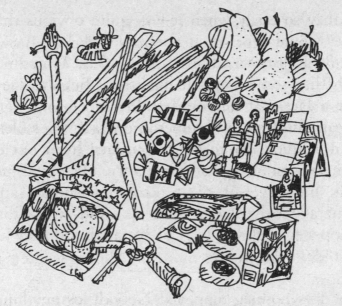

biscuits and sweets, things brought into school for swapsies, Gowso's violin strings, combs, Legweak's keyring with the tiny torch attached, crisps and cartons of juice.

Jimmy Zest read out the list.

"Right. If anything from this page is lost, stolen or broken, I promise that I will provide the money for a new one. That's very good value for only ten pence a week."

One thoughtful person stood back from this sudden new craze to get insured. Penny Brown wondered how on earth sensible people like Mandy could be so stupid as to part with their money so easily when it was quite obvious that they would never see it again. Never!

Penny Brown admired Jimmy Zest sometimes – he had some very fine qualities – but she knew for a fact that he could suddenly become very mean. Just wait until something was lost or stolen, and let them try to get the money for it out of Jimmy Zest. They had no chance. He would just talk his way out of it, keep the money and generally behave like a miser. And when that happened they wouldn't be so much in love with the idea of insurance.

For days, nothing happened. Nobody lost anything, nothing was stolen or broken. Pens, apples, fruit juice, crisps – things which you could normally rely on to vanish once in a while – these things refused to disappear now that they were insured. It was all very disappointing, especially for Penny Brown.

There was some excitement on Friday morning when Shorty lost his dinner ticket. Jimmy Zest made him take off his jacket, empty his pockets and search in his socks, and Penny Brown said: "Why don't you make him take all his clothes off, Zesty, then you'll be sure?" – but the ticket didn't turn up. Then Miss Quick, their teacher, brought it into class and said that it had been picked up in the playground.

"Noel, please take care of your property in future," Miss Quick said to Shorty.

"I wasn't worried, Miss," Shorty told her. "I had it insured."

"Don't be silly, you can't insure a fiddly thing like a dinner ticket. Books out, please."

In this way an uneventful week went by. When Monday morning came again, Jimmy Zest collected in ten more pence from each of his clients.

"That's a whole pound the miser's got," Penny Brown pointed out. She swore that you could actually hear the loot chinking in his pockets when he walked.

Then, at last, something happened. On Tuesday Mandy Taylor announced that her yogurt was missing.

She made the others look in her schoolbag.

"See? I had it in there. It's absolutely gone."

"Just like my Waggon Wheel," said Legweak.

Shorty suggested that maybe she'd left it at home.

"I did not, Shorty, I had it with me in English. I said to it 'Soon I'm going to eat you' and I wouldn't have been talking to it if I'd left it at

home, would I? It was a wild-fruit yogurt with raspberries in it."

Penny Brown looked about her to see if Jimmy Zest was in the room but, as usual, he was somewhere else when he was needed most.

"Mandy, don't you worry. Listen, everybody, she'll get another one free out of Zesty's insurance."

"Do you think so?" Mandy didn't sound too sure.

"Certainly you will. Didn't you see his pockets yesterday? Bulging! That's what he's got that money for – to protect your yogurt. Let's go and find him."

So they all headed off towards the library where

the elusive Jimmy Zest had last been seen. They spotted him behind a bookcase.

Typical, thought Penny Brown. He was always reading. Always trying to find out how the world works. "Listen, Mandy," she said – for Mandy was rather timid, and sometimes needed protecting – "you be firm. He'll try to wriggle out of this, don't be soft with him."

"I'll not."

"Remember, he owes you money."

Nodding grimly, Mandy Taylor led the way into the library. When Gowso and Knuckles and Shorty, and Legweak and Penny Brown and Mandy Taylor gathered round him in a circle, Jimmy Zest calmly closed his book on origami and listened with great sympathy while Mandy explained how she had lost her yogurt.

He said it was a shame.

"But are you sure you brought it into school, Amanda?"

"Zesty," said Penny Brown, "she's one hundred per cent positive she brought it into school."

"She was talking to it in English," said Shorty, and Legweak the wit added: "Yogurts can't speak French."

"Shut up, Legweak, this is serious." And Penny Brown poked Mandy in the ribs until she spoke.

"I'm claiming insurance, Zesty," Mandy said.

In the quiet of the library, all eyes now rested on Jimmy Zest as he opened his jotter and turned to the page where he had written down the list of things which were insured. His monotonous voice began, "Pens, dinner tickets, violin strings, crisps – it doesn't say anything about yogurt here, Amanda." And he shook his head sadly as if he was truly downhearted himself.

"But it says break biscuits," Mandy pointed out anxiously.

"I know it does. A break biscuit is a break biscuit and a yogurt is a yogurt. They are not the same thing."

This silenced Mandy Taylor completely. She badly wanted to say something, for she did not wish to be soft with Jimmy Zest but, as Gowso quietly pointed out, you couldn't argue with the fact that a yogurt was a yogurt and a break biscuit was a break biscuit.

Gowso ought to have known that Penny Brown could argue with anything.

"A break biscuit," she declared, "means *any* goodie you bring in for your break and even if it doesn't, Mandy wants her money back, you mean snook."

"You shouldn't lose your temper, Penelope."

"It's my temper, Zesty, I'll lose it for ever if I feel like it."

The situation had become rather serious. Shorty, who was easily influenced by Penny Brown, began to look quite aggressive, while Knuckles, his twin, took his hands out of his pockets and folded his arms. Usually, this was a bad sign for somebody. Legweak wondered how Zesty would get out of this one and Gowso stood hugging the case of his violin, looking thoughtful. As for Mandy Taylor, she played her part to perfection by staring down at her feet exactly like a downtrodden victim.

From an inside pocket of his blazer, Jimmy Zest produced one of his many writing implements. He added the word YOGURT to the list in his jotter.

"There. All yogurt is insured from this second onwards. That should solve the problem. Please keep your schoolbag buckled in future, Amanda." And with that he picked up his book on origami and marched smartly out of the library.

Shorty didn't understand what had happened. Had Mandy Taylor been given the money for a new carton of yogurt in some mysterious way? Was it compensation?

"Not at all!" snapped Penny Brown. "Didn't I say so? Didn't I tell you? You can't argue with

Jimmy Zest, you've got no chance of getting money out of that miser. You should have known better, Mandy."

Mandy Taylor was not the only person in the library who looked a little crestfallen after this attack, for it seemed that perhaps Penny Brown had been right all along. After all, there wasn't really much difference between a yogurt and a break biscuit, and there wasn't much point in paying out ten whole pence a week for insurance that didn't work.

It was obvious from their faces that Jimmy Zest might not get away with it so easily the next time.

Just before home time, Miss Quick embarrassed poor old Gowso and made him cringe in his seat.

"Philip," she said – his real name was Philip McGowan – "Would you play something for us on your violin? One of your pieces for the concert would end the day very nicely."

The whole class received this idea with shouts of approval, especially when Miss Quick added that she would let them off homework if Gowso would agree.

But Gowso huddled in his desk like a person trying to shrink.

"I haven't done enough practice, Miss."

"Go ahead, Gowso," Shorty shouted, "sure it's only us."

"Miss, I haven't got a stand for my music."

Miss Quick solved that problem by appointing Mandy Taylor to be his music stand. So the reluctant Gowso took his fiddle out of his case, then his bow, and started into one of his pieces. Every time he pushed the bow his eyebrows went up, and every time he pulled the bow his eyebrows came down again. When he played the twiddly bits in his tune, his eyes blinked.

Although Gowso made some mistakes, Miss Quick was very impressed by his performance,

and allowed Jimmy Zest to lead the class in a round of applause. While this was happening, Penny Brown hissed at Mandy Taylor and threw her a note.

> Your yogurt had fruit in it.
> *Fruit.* He insures all fruit.
> Get him after school.

Mandy nodded over to Penny as Miss Quick began to speak.

"Oh, that was nice, Philip. People don't appreciate how wonderful it is to be able to play a musical instrument. Well done."

"Good old Gowso," Shorty called out when the bell ended the school day, "no homework tonight!"

Miss Quick let her class out row by row, which was unfortunate for Mandy Taylor and Penny Brown. Jimmy Zest's row got out first and there was no sign of him in the corridor when the girls looked for him.

"Just you wait until tomorrow, Zesty," said Penny Brown.

Next morning something really peculiar happened even before lessons started. Gowso came into the classroom, went straight to a corner and sat there hugging his violin. There was a wicked scowl on his face. He wouldn't speak to anybody. Legweak came in and shouted, "Hiya Gowso" across the room, but the friendly greeting had no effect. Gowso continued to scowl.

Penny Brown said, in a whisper, "Shorty, I think he's been crying."

"Why?"

"Look at his face, it's all blotchy."

"What's he crying for?"

"*I* don't know, Shorty, how would *I* know?"

However, she was determined to find out. It didn't seem right that he should sit there like a miserable drip, so she marched up to him.

"Right, Gowso, what's the matter with you? It's not the end of the world, you know."

"Leave me alone."

"Gowso, we're your friends, OK? You can't just ignore us for nothing." Penny noticed that his violin case had a long score down it. "Is it your fiddle? It is, it's your fiddle. There's something wrong with your fiddle."

Not many people could resist Penny Brown when she was determined to be helpful. Eventually she bullied Gowso into admitting that he had been stopped on the way to school, and that yes, something was wrong with his violin.

Here was dramatic news to start off the day! Knuckles and the others – including Jimmy Zest, who had just come in – gathered round as Gowso opened the case of his violin. It looked perfectly all right, Penny had expected to see it in bits. Then Gowso held up the bow of his violin. The strings of the bow had been cut through and it was ruined.

The story came out. On the way to school Gowso had been stopped by two bigger boys near the shops, and they had forced him to open his case. They didn't do Gowso or his violin any harm but, for a joke, they cut through the hairs of his bow with a penknife.

Immediately, Knuckles demanded some information. What did the boys look like? How old were they? What school were they from?

"Nobody's going to pick on one of our friends and get away with it," he said murderously, "are they, Shorty?"

Shorty, like his brother, began to make noises of war.

"Oh, shut up you two," Penny Brown said. "It's too late for that now. Gowso needs a new bow."

Poor old Gowso's eyes watered. He looked such a picture of misery that Mandy Taylor came up with an inspired idea.

"I know. He could get insurance! Zesty'll give you insurance for a new one, won't you, Zesty?"

It seemed like a great idea. None of the others had thought about insurance.

"Actually," said Jimmy Zest, "his bow wasn't insured, only his strings."

Penny Brown grabbed Gowso's bow and shook it rather ominously in Jimmy Zest's direction. The loose strands danced at both ends of the bow like a complicated whip.

"What do you think those are, Zesty? Those

are strings too, or I'm from outer space."

Perhaps Jimmy Zest realized that this time, he would have to give way. Perhaps he really felt sorry for Gowso.

"OK. Insurance will be paid," he agreed, turning to the page where he kept his accounts, "but there's not much money."

"That doesn't matter," said Penny Brown quickly, "you agreed to pay. Anyway, a fiddly old bow couldn't cost much."

If they expected Gowso to be cheered up by the news that he would get insurance, they were wrong.

"It costs a hundred pounds to have a bow strung," he said mournfully.

All conversation ceased. Nobody could believe it. Penny Brown said "Flute!" Even a miser like Jimmy Zest couldn't come up with that kind of money.

"What's it made of, Gowso?" Legweak wanted to know. "Pure gold?"

"Horsehair!" snapped Gowso. "Hair from a horse's tail." And he stormed off to sit at his table, alone.

His friends refused to give up on the problem so easily. Legweak said that they should advertise in the paper. Shorty pointed out that if you could buy oxtail soup, why not a horsetail, which confused everybody.

Jimmy Zest said: "Look, the wooden bit of the bow is all right. Maybe, if we knew where there was a horse . . ."

"Brilliant, Zesty," said Penny Brown. "Just walk up to it and say excuse me, Mr Horse could I have a bit of your tail for Gowso's bow. That's really bright."

Luckily Miss Quick came into the room and put an end to this rather wild talk. In no time at all she had them lined up to march down to the gym for assembly.

Halfway down the corridor Shorty heard the voice of Jimmy Zest talking softly in his ear.

"Shorty, I know where there's a horse."

It took a while for Shorty to work out what Zesty had in mind. Then, at last, the penny dropped. And when it did, there was a gleam in Shorty's eye, too.

Jimmy Zest and his friends the Alexander twins were experts when it came to finding their way about their own neighbourhood.

Not only did they know all the streets and the short cuts through the streets as well as any taxi driver or postman, but also, they knew things about their neighbourhood which taxi drivers and postmen did not necessarily know. They knew, for example, that you got great wood for your bonfire down in Mercer's Wood.

In order to get to Mercer's Wood you crossed Mercer's field, and in Mercer's field there lived a dozy old grey horse which did nothing all day but stretch its neck down to the short grass and swish its long, lovely tail.

After school Jimmy Zest, Shorty and Knuckles decided to pay Mercer's horse a visit. They agreed to let Legweak come with them, mainly because he volunteered to bring along his mum's big dressmaking scissors.

And they needed scissors for what Jimmy Zest had in mind.

When the field came into view Shorty said, "I hope these scissors are sharp, Legweak. If you hurt this thing it'll hit you a boot with its big back feet and that'll be the end of you."

Legweak stopped in his tracks. "Me? Hey wait a minute. *I'm* not doing this. I'm only bringing the scissors."

Knuckles took the scissors from him. With six quick clips he snipped the heads off six nettles by the roadside.

"Like razors," he said, satisfied. Then he paid

attention while Jimmy Zest outlined his plan of action.

Although he did not like to admit it, Legweak was beginning to feel just a little bit nervous. By the time he arrived at the field and caught sight of the horse, he was more than a little bit nervous. Like most people he'd seen hundreds of horses. Almost every one of them had been under the control of a cowboy, or an Indian, or a jockey in a race. But this great, heavy lump of a real-life horse was not on television, it was standing in Mercer's field and it had feet the size of turnips.

Legweak said uneasily: "Know what I think? I think we should ask Mr Mercer if we can have some hairs off his horse."

This idea had not occurred to Knuckles or Shorty, or even to Jimmy Zest, but to please Legweak – who owned the scissors, after all – they agreed.

"Where does he live?" asked Knuckles. Shorty pointed to a small bungalow across the road. It was the only house in sight.

"Probably over there."

So they went up the path, and Shorty knocked on the door. An elderly lady opened it.

"Mrs Mercer," said Shorty, "would you let us have some hairs out of your horse's tail?"

The lady – who was *not* Mrs Mercer – stared in the direction pointed out by Shorty's finger. Across the road, the grey horse poked its nose through the bars of an iron gate and tore up some grass. It looked very peaceful.

The lady didn't answer Shorty for a moment or two. She seemed very surprised.

"It's not my horse, son."

"Oh."

"It's not even my field."

"Oh," Shorty said again.

"What have you got in your hand, son?"

"Dressmaking scissors," Knuckles informed her.

"Oh I see." Suddenly the elderly lady wasn't there any more, and her door was shut.

And now, as if they had been given permission to go right ahead, the twins crossed the road to the iron gate, where Mercer's horse stopped munching to stare at them out of one bulging brown eye.

"Nice horse," Shorty said to it. The tail swished.

Jimmy Zest was very encouraged by that tail. Not only was it extremely thick and bushy, but it also reached all the way down to the horse's ankles. Clearly there were enough hairs here to fix the bows for an entire orchestra of fiddles, and there would still be plenty left over for the horse to scare flies with.

Cautiously, Knuckles slipped back the bolt in the gate. "We want no sudden moves," he said over his shoulder. Then he crept into the field, scissors at the ready.

Jimmy Zest, as usual, gave the instructions. Legweak attended to the gate and kept watch along the road, just in case. Shorty's job, which he now did very carefully, was to approach the eating end of the horse with a handful of especially juicy grass. Knuckles, meanwhile, crept up from behind with the scissors open and ready to snip. The role of Jimmy Zest, the general, was to encourage the others.

Legweak could hardly bear to watch, even from the safety of the road.

"Knuckles," he said, "watch you don't hurt it."

Beside the horse, the twins looked like midgets.

"How could I hurt it," came the answer. "It's only hair I'm cutting. It's just like you and me going to the barber's."

At first Zesty's plan worked really well. Mercer's horse nuzzled the grass at the end of Shorty's stiff arm, and seemed tempted.

"Breathe up its nostrils, Shorty," advised Jimmy Zest.

No way. If you were close enough to a horse to breathe up its nose, the horse was close enough to you to bite your head off – so ran Shorty's thinking.

"What do you think I am, Zesty – a looper?"

"Stroke it, then," hissed Knuckles from the back end, "I'm not close enough yet."

But the horse did not wish to be stroked. It trotted away sideways, and its tail swished up and round in a circle as if it knew something was about to happen.

"It knows, it knows," Legweak said from the gate, "it's getting suspicious, it's getting suspicious."

He wished he was somewhere else. Anywhere else. "Shut up, Legweak, what do you know about horses?" said Knuckles, as if he trimmed a dozen horses' tails a day. "Talk to it, Shorty."

"There's a good horse, there's a good horse," said Shorty. "Do you not want my lovely grass?"

While the horse was making up its mind about the lovely grass, Knuckles rushed in and attacked its tail with Legweak's mum's dressmaking scissors.

Simultaneously, the horse's lips seemed to shudder so violently that Shorty had a terrifying view of its enormous yellow teeth. As the horse's head plunged down, Shorty imagined that those teeth were about to take lumps out of him, which is why he turned and sprinted and cleared three strands of barbed-wire fence as if it wasn't there, and Legweak, scared witless by the horse's high whinny, let go of the iron gate and raced to the far side of the road for safety.

But Mercer's horse was not interested in him. It had whipped round, and now stood snuffling and snorting at Knuckles, who had a piece of its tail in one hand and scissors in the other.

Shorty let out a scream.

"Run for it, Knuckles!" Unfortunately Knuckles could not move, for fear had immobilized him.

It was the horse who ran. It wheeled away towards the gate, which had been abandoned by

Legweak and now lay wide open. Within seconds the horse was galloping down the public road with its hooves clattering and the remains of its tail streaming out behind it in the wind.

Legweak emerged from behind a tree, shouting, "It's got away, it's got away, it's got away."

He stood repeating this in the middle of the road like a demented parrot – until he realized that Shorty and Knuckles and Zesty were galloping too, but in the opposite direction from the horse.

Now, Legweak began to run. It was as if someone had wound him up tight and let him go – his legs carried him along and he was just a passenger.

For sure, he was thinking, Mr Mercer would prosecute them for trespassing and losing his horse and stealing part of its bushy big tail. "It wasn't my fault," shouted Legweak as he ran along. "I only held the gate." But the scissors! They would accuse him of supplying the scissors. Oh, if only they'd used hedge-clippers instead and left him at home. Truly, this was without doubt the worst trouble he'd ever been in unless . . . unless a miracle happened and Mercer's stupid horse turned and came back to its field like a homing pigeon.

This thought calmed Legweak down a bit. Surely a horse had more brains than a pigeon? But he kept running.

The word RASPBERRY caused an argument in school the following morning.

Penny Brown was involved. So were Jimmy Zest, Mandy Taylor and her missing carton of yogurt.

"It had raspberries in it. Fruit!" cried Penny Brown with the confidence of one who knows that she is absolutely right. "You insure apples, oranges and all fruit, Jimmy Zest. You owe Mandy money for her raspberry yogurt."

"No."

"Yes!"

"Penelope, yogurt is milk. Sour milk."

"It was wild-fruit yogurt. Wild fruit, wild fruit."

By this time Jimmy Zest had his back to the

board and could retreat no further. He was about to call for a dictionary to help him fight his case against Penny Brown when Shorty and Knuckles burst through the classroom door at ten to nine as if a holiday had just been declared.

"Hey, hey, hey," Knuckles shouted, "you'll never guess what we got."

"Gowso," yelled Shorty, "look – hairs for your fiddle's bow."

Yogurt was forgotten. Knuckles held the strands of coarse hair – which he had knotted at one end to keep them together – above his head in triumph.

"There it is," Shorty said with pride. "Horse tail."

"Where did you get it?" Mandy Taylor foolishly asked him.

"Off a giraffe. Right, Gowso, get out your bow and we'll tie it on."

However, this was not to be. Gowso reached into his violin case and brought out a bow which looked perfectly sound in every respect. His dad had managed to get one from a man in his work who had played the violin years ago.

Penny Brown thought it was a shame.

"Of course I'm glad you've got a bow, Gowso. But could you not keep Shorty's tail for spares?"

Then Legweak, who had been very quiet,

hissed from the door that Miss Quick was coming down the corridor.

She was in an absolutely terrifying mood. Her lips were thin with rage, and she looked as though she would keep the whole world in until six o'clock at least. Mandy Taylor couldn't look at her eyes in case they shrivelled her up.

Then Miss Quick spoke. "I want the pupils of this class to know that I have just come from the headmaster's office."

Flute! thought Penny Brown, such a way to start the day. Usually she said Good Morning or something pleasant like that.

"Noel Alexander, Nicholas Alexander — stand up!"

Shorty stood up. Knuckles stood up.

"Who was with you yesterday?"

"Me, Miss?" Knuckles inquired innocently.

"Yesterday, Miss?" Shorty asked nicely.

"Who was with you yesterday at Mercer's field? You were seen. Or do you really believe that you are invisible?"

"No, Miss," said Shorty.

"At any rate *that's* a relief."

Suddenly Miss Quick appeared to lose interest in the twins.

"Philip McGowan, what is that in your hand?"

Gowso turned scarlet.

"A bit of a horse's tail, Miss."

Legweak did not turn scarlet. He was the colour of chalk as he rose to his feet.

"I was at Mercer's field, Miss."

"You too. Was anyone else from this dreadful class involved in yesterday's incident? I mean anyone – in any way?"

A chair creaked in the silence. Through her fingers Penny Brown saw that it was Jimmy Zest.

"I think you might say it was my idea, Miss Quick. Could I please . . ."

"Your idea. It wouldn't surprise me, not one bit, I know you and your ideas, James Zest. You five boys will go now to Mr Wilson's office, where he is waiting to interview you about a *horse*!"

And straight away she marched to the door of the classroom. She ripped it open so quickly that the papers on her desk rustled in the draught.

As the boys left the room, Penny Brown's heart was thumping like mad. She felt sorry for them of course, but flute! was she relieved that she hadn't been with them.

Snails in their heavy shells could have crawled up the long corridor to Mr Wilson's office more quickly than Jimmy Zesty and his friends. Legweak, who could not forget that he had supplied the scissors, would rather have faced the horse in Mercer's field at that moment.

As for Gowso, he kept saying, "But I wasn't there. I wasn't even there." He flung the horse's tail to the ground and refused to carry it a step further.

So Shorty tucked the piece of tail down his trousers.

"Might come in useful sometime," he said. "Cheer up, Gowso."

"It's all right for you, Shorty," grumbled Gowso – by which he meant that Shorty had been to the headmaster's office many times before.

Mr Wilson made them stand in silence in front of his big desk. While they were waiting there for something to happen, the tail of the horse – the end with the knot in it – came sliding out of Shorty's left trouser leg, and rested on his shoe.

Gowso couldn't help himself.

"I wasn't even there, sir," he blurted out.

"You will be quiet," Mr Wilson told him. "First I will have my say."

After Mr Wilson had picked up the horse tail from Shorty's shoe, he said quite a lot. He went through all the horrible things which might have happened because of their stupidity. The horse might have been killed on the open road, had they thought of that? No. The horse might have knocked down a cyclist or a pedestrian, had they thought of that? No. Had they thought about the damage a runaway horse could do to property or to people or to itself? No, they hadn't thought at all, Mr Wilson said. Brains were wasted on them. By sheer good luck the owner of the horse had managed to track it down and persuade it into a horsebox. They were responsible, Mr Wilson said, for a great deal of worry and inconvenience, and what would their parents say if they knew about this?

Nobody answered him. Knuckles did some

shuffling and Legweak felt sure that there would be talk about scissors any second.

"I don't understand," Mr Wilson said. "Why did you attack that poor horse, which was only minding its own business in its own field?"

He seemed to be staring at Jimmy Zest, but it was Shorty who replied.

"You see, sir, we wanted to fix the bow of Gowso's fiddle. A couple of rowdies broke it on him. You see Zesty sells insurance, sir."

"He sells what?"

"Insurance. Well, there wasn't enough money in the insurance so Zesty said what we needed was a horse. We didn't mean to hurt the horse, sir. Knuckles said it would be just like going to the barber's."

"I only held the gate," Legweak butted in, now that it was possible to speak.

"I wasn't even there," Gowso said again.

"That's right," Knuckles backed him up. "He wasn't there."

Mr Wilson told Gowso that he could go, and Gowso left the office rather more quickly than he had come in. Then the headmaster turned to Jimmy Zest.

"Insurance. Did he say that you sell insurance?"

"Yes, sir."

"What kind of things do you insure?"

"Yogurt, pencils, crisps, things like that."

"Also dinner tickets," Knuckles added, to be helpful. "It only costs you ten pence a week."

The headmaster stroked his moustache. It was such a thick moustache that it seemed to block up his nose.

"You mean . . . you actually have the audacity to take money off people?"

"Yes, sir."

"For insurance? And they give you money?"

"They do, sir."

For a moment Mr Wilson seemed slightly amused behind his huge moustache, but not for long.

"I don't know which is worse, chasing horses or financial fraud. You will return all the money to your clients, Mr Zest. And furthermore, I would like to point out to you children that this piece of horse tail" – he waggled it in front of their eyes – "would have been of no use whatever to you. It takes a highly skilled craftsman to string a violin bow. Now, I will see you all later today, when we shall discuss what punishment you deserve. You will certainly write letters of apology to the gentleman who owns the horse. That will do for a start."

He flung the tail of Mercer's horse into the wastepaper basket and told them to go.

The boys were late home from school that day.

So, too, were Mandy Taylor and Penny Brown, who decided to walk home by the road that ran alongside Mercer's field – a detour which added over a mile to their journey.

Of course they had plenty to talk about, especially when they thought how it must have sickened Jimmy Zest to hand back all his insurance money. Miss Quick had stood over him and personally supervised the whole business, which had shocked her. She said it was extortion. Penny Brown thought this was a lovely word.

"I hope you've learned your lesson about that miser, Mandy," she said.

Mandy didn't answer. She was staring at Mercer's famous horse, which had suddenly come into view. It looked so peaceful, champing away at its own grass. Then it gave a snort, and raised its head to stare out of one bulging brown eye at the two strangers. It stood motionless, except for its tail, and when its tail swished, like a warning, you could hardly help noticing that part of it was missing.

Not for a hundred pounds would Penny Brown have ventured into that field.

"Mandy," she said, "you've got to admit it, they were really quite brave."

Mandy Taylor didn't have to admit any such thing. She thought of her stolen yogurt.

"If you ask me they were really quite stupid," she said bluntly.

- 4 -

Under the Rhubarb

On Saturday morning, Gowso and Shorty and Jimmy Zest passed the shops on their way to the park.

Shorty was messing about with what he called a hand grenade.

"It's lethal, Gowso, lethal!" shouted Shorty. And he threw the hand grenade dangerously high into the air, and stood underneath it with his hands cupped.

"Am I going to drop it, am I doing to drop it? If I drop it we're goners, Gowso!"

Actually, the lethal hand grenade was a large fir cone from a tree in Mercer's Wood, and Shorty caught it a foot from the ground. When Gowso wiped his brow with relief, Shorty grinned.

"Never worry, Gowso – I didn't have the pin out."

While these two idiots diced with death, Jimmy Zest read a notice in the sweetie shop window. This was easily the most interesting notice he had read in a long time, which is why he whistled Gowso and Shorty over to have a look at it:

> Tortoise lost. A very special
> pet. Please return if found to
> George Hawthorne – £50 reward.

"It's a joke," Shorty said at once. "Somebody has added on a nought. Only a looper would pay that kind of money for a tortoise. Right, Zesty?"

Zesty could not give Shorty an answer, for he was travelling up the road with the speed of something which has just been launched, and Gowso wasn't far behind him.

"Hey! Wait for me, you two."

Shorty tossed his unexploded grenade into a litter bin and raced after them.

Mandy Taylor sprinted along Penny Brown's garden path until she came to a shaky old shed which had a sign above the door. The sign said: ROSE COTTAGE.

This was their private hut. The girls had fixed it up themselves and this Saturday morning they had planned to wash the windows and put up purple curtains. But that was before Mandy had seen the extraordinary notice about Mr Hawthorne's valuable missing tortoise.

Penny Brown just gasped when she heard what it was worth.

"Fifty? Pounds?"

"That's what it said. Five and nought."

"Flute!"

For a moment or two Penny Brown dreamed about what she could buy with fifty pounds if her daddy didn't force her to put it in the bank: then she and Mandy flew out of Rose Cottage to find out more about this.

They didn't have to fly far, for Mr and Mrs Hawthorne lived on the same road as the Browns, three doors up.

Mrs Hawthorne opened the door.

"Don't speak, girls – I know! You saw the notice in the shop window. Oh, the power of advertising, you are my third lot of visitors this morning. I doubt if you'll find her, Penny. Poor Mabel."

"Was Mabel your tortoise's name, Mrs Hawthorne?"

It was. And three weeks ago Mabel had wakened up from her long winter sleep and had wandered away into the big wide world. Mrs

Hawthorne said they had searched everywhere, but Mabel must have escaped into the golf course which ran along the back of the house. "She's a very big tortoise, girls," finished Mrs Hawthorne, "as big as a dinner-plate. George has had her for thirty-two years, would you believe that? Well, you get very fond of a thing when you've had it for thirty-two years."

Penny promised her that they would do what they could to find her. As they came through the Hawthornes' gate, Mandy Taylor still had not recovered from her astonishment.

"Do you realize something? That tortoise is older than my mother. How can it live that long?"

"Because that's the way they're made, Mandy. Did you hear what Mrs Hawthorne said. She's had people in to see her already. I bet you any money that'll be Jimmy Zest. He'll find Mabel, the lucky snook."

"Or Nicholas Alexander," said Mandy in alarm. "Oh, I hope he doesn't, we'll never hear the end of it."

Nicholas Alexander and Legweak were, at that very moment, sitting on an old mattress which they had found along the edge of the golf course. They had been searching for half an hour already, and Legweak had come to a conclusion.

He pointed to the greenhouse in the garden next door to the Hawthornes'.

"It's in there," he said quietly. "It's in the greenhouse."

"How do you know?"

"I'm trying to think like a tortoise. They like heat, you see."

"Well what are you waiting for?" said Knuckles.

Carefully, Legweak eased his skinny body through the gap where the hedge was thinnest and dragged himself up the garden by digging in the points of his elbows. When he reached the greenhouse door he slid it open and crawled in on his tummy. On the dirt floor he saw twenty or thirty plastic buckets containing young tomato plants. While Legweak poked his nose among the foliage of this small forest, a heavy foot came down on his back, pinning him to the ground. He knew that he'd been got.

"Oh no," said Legweak.

"Oh yes, yes," said a man's deep voice.

Legweak thought that he should probably say something.

"Mister, I was only looking for a tortoise."

"Any luck?"

"No, sir."

"What a shame. You know, it must be some tortoise if it can open greenhouse doors and shut them again behind it. Is it a super-tortoise?"

"I don't think so, sir."

The man had a spray gun in his hand. He bent down so that Legweak had a good view of it.

"If I see you in my garden again I'll give you a squirt of this here, which is great stuff. It destroys all pests known to man. Out you go."

Legweak tried to prise himself off the ground, but that foot kept him where he was.

"No, no," the man said, "the way you came in. Go out the way you came in."

So Legweak crawled on his stomach all the way

down the garden path to the back hedge.

"You know," the man said in a complimentary way, "you would make a very good tortoise yourself if you'd a shell on your back." And he showed the spray gun to Legweak one more time so that he would remember.

Knuckles had seen and heard it all. The sight of Legweak-the-Tortoise, clawing his way back through the hedge on soggy elbows and knees – it was just too much for him. He rolled about the mattress kicking his feet in the air.

"I don't think it's that funny, Knuckles."

That made Knuckles worse. He sounded as though he would injure himself laughing and the mattress went bang bang!

Just before Saturday lunch-time, Penny Brown phoned Jimmy Zest with an invitation.

"Zesty, have you heard about the tortoise? You haven't found it yet, have you?"

"Not yet, Penelope."

Oh good, thought Penny. But he would find it, she was sure of that – some stroke of genius would occur to him and the fifty-pound reward would be his.

"Zesty, Mandy and I want you to come over to our private hut in my garden and we can all make plans to look for it together. Bring Shorty if you like but not Knuckles. But you'll have to agree to split the reward, Zesty. That'll be about twelve pounds each, OK?"

A slight hesitation occurred at the other end of the phone.

"I didn't know you had a private hut."

"You can't expect to know everything that happens in the world, Zesty."

"OK, it's agreed."

When Jimmy Zest arrived at Rose Cottage about fifteen minutes later, Shorty was with him. And Gowso.

"Who invited you, Philip McGowan?" inquired Penny Brown.

The look on her face suggested that Gowso had invited himself, and that he'd no business to.

"Well, you'll just have to sit on the floor, we've only got four logs."

Since Gowso was in no position to make a nuisance of himself, he accepted a seat on the cold stone floor. Then Jimmy Zest cleared his throat, and began to make known some facts about tortoises.

"They're reptiles," he said. "They lay eggs. They go back two hundred million years, which makes them very old, right?"

"Ancient, even," said Shorty.

"Tortoises come into this country from hot countries like Morocco, that's why they mostly die. It's illegal to import them nowadays. And they like a sandy terrain."

"What's that?"

"Sand, Shorty, sand," said Penny Brown. "Where would you get sand around here?"

Mandy Taylor stood up. Her eyes were shining as if a light had come on inside her head.

"I know, I know! The golf course. The bunkers." Penny Brown came to the end of her log and almost clonked Gowso's head with her knee.

"Zesty – she is right. Mandy, you are brilliant, there's sand in the bunkers. That's where Mabel must be!"

They left Rose Cottage in such a hurry that the whole thing creaked and quaked. Climbing the fence into the golf course, Shorty did a quick sum in his head: "Hey, five into fifty goes ten times and none over."

"Spot the genius," Mandy Taylor said under her breath.

After thirty minutes they had searched fourteen bunkers of sand for a hole which might have been made by a runaway tortoise. They had no luck at all until Gowso began to shriek and point with both hands.

"I've found an egg. An egg, an egg!" he cried, and Penny Brown led the charge to see Gowso's egg, which lay partially buried in sand. Carefully, Penny picked it up between fingers and thumb.

It didn't feel like an egg.

"Calm down, Gowso, you goof," she said, "tortoises don't lay golf balls."

After this ridiculous false alarm they searched some more for big Mabel, but soon, reluctantly, they had to face the fact that she had made a very thorough job of disappearing. Shorty said she was definitely a goner – he reckoned she had been squashed by a lorry while slowly crossing the road.

Later in the afternoon two patient, leg-weary bounty-hunters trudged up the side of the golf course laden with the results of their day's labour.

One of them was Knuckles, the other was Legweak. And they were still searching. Although they hadn't managed to lay their hands on the missing fifty-pound tortoise, they had collected up a spongy old mattress and several other items which might come in useful one day. The mattress, for example, would burn when it dried out.

They were passing the end of Penny Brown's

garden when Knuckles held up his hand like an Indian scout.

"Do you hear voices, Legweak?"

"Yip."

As quietly as possible, they picked a path through the tangle of briars and undergrowth to Penny Brown's back fence, where Knuckles put his ear to the planks of a tumbledown shack.

He settled a finger over his lips. "Shhh!" Penny Brown was talking.

"OK, has everybody got their money in? If your money's not in you can't come to the feast. Let's make a list. Shorty – what are you having?"

Knuckles and Legweak heard a silence while Shorty did some thinking.

"I'll have a Walnut Whip, a packet of salt 'n' vinegar, and a packet of something chewy as well."

"Wine gums," suggested Jimmy Zest.

"Can you afford all that, Shorty?"

"Certainly."

"We'll need white lemonade," said Mandy Taylor. "I just love the sound of fizz."

"It's rotten when it gets up your nose."

"Then wear a clothes peg on your nose, Gowso."

They went on and on about what they were going to eat. Just to listen to them made Legweak's tummy rumble with jealousy. Knuckles couldn't stand it, he tapped on the back of the hut and shouted out:

"Can we come too?"

All conversation immediately ceased inside the hut. Then Knuckles and Legweak saw a bush moving, and Penny Brown's head poked through.

"Who do you think you're spying on, Legweak?"

"We're not spying, we're looking for big Mabel."

"Well she's halfway back to Morocco – cheerio."

Knuckles, when he spoke, tried to make

himself sound very humble.

"We'll let you have a mattress for your hut if you let us come to your feast."

The last thing on earth Penny Brown wanted was his mattress. Probably somebody had died on it, or something.

"Look. It's only for members of Rose Cottage. We can't let you in because the girls are outnumbered already. That's just the way it is, Knuckles."

Curiously enough, Knuckles didn't cause trouble. There was none of his usual bad temper when people said "No" to him.

"That's OK," he said, "you don't want us. Rose Cottage is a dump. Let's go, Legweak."

Once Knuckles got his feet clear of the long grass, he broke into a run. Legweak couldn't understand the sudden urgency, or why they seemed to be heading for Mercer's Wood.

"Hang about, Knuckles," he complained, "we're supposed to be looking for a tortoise."

Knuckles gave a rather menacing laugh. "Forget the tortoise. We need ammunition."

Inside the privacy of Rose Cottage, a Saturday feast was about to happen. Mandy Taylor, whose mum was an excellent hostess, had taken the trouble to slice a Mars bar into ten pieces – two for each person. These, when passed around, signified the official opening of the occasion.

"You may now eat, everyone," Penny Brown said grandly.

Before they actually tasted anything, various kinds of swops were negotiated. Gowso worried whether half a Fry's Cream was worth half a Crunchie while Jimmy Zest dispensed lemonade from the bottle into paper cups.

"Very fancy," said Shorty.

There was a sharp WHACK. Something quite heavy hit the roof of Rose Cottage. Shorty stood up.

CLUNK.

"There it is again!" shouted Gowso.

Some of his crisps spilled on to the floor and lay there unnoticed, for the whacks and the clunks were coming thickly now, accompanied all the while by the rhythm of a distant voice calling: "Dat-dat-dat-dat-dat. Dat-dat-dat-dat-dat."

Shorty threw himself to the floor, for he recognized that sound.

"It's machine-gun fire," he yelled.

Penny Brown finished her fizzy lemonade in one gulp and whipped back a purple curtain to see Legweak running for cover through her daddy's vegetable patch. Shorty, meanwhile, had grabbed a brush, and returned rapid fire through a crack in the door.

"Dat-dat-dat-dat-dat. Got you, Legweak."

"You never did!" came a faint reply from behind the rhubarb leaves.

All the while, Rose Cottage was being bombarded with missiles from the vicinity of a small quince tree.

"Knuckles!" screamed Gowso, "he's got grenades!"

Shorty, whose head was hanging out of the door, had to retreat when a grenade almost scored a direct hit on him. He came into the hut backwards, feet first, walking on his elbows.

"We're in trouble," he said desperately. "They've got us pinned down. Crossfire, you see."

"Have they," said Penny Brown.

Crossfire or no crossfire, she came racing out of Rose Cottage with the long-handled yard brush in her hands and as she ran, she yelled: "You are for it this time, Nicholas Alexander!"

Knuckles saw her coming. The sound of her voice and the mean look on her face convinced him that Penny Brown meant business with that brush. He decided to evacuate the premises with all possible speed. Even as these thoughts were running through his mind, Knuckles came to an intelligent conclusion: he would never make it. She was almost on top of him and the brush was rising.

So he threw a hand grenade and hit her in the face. Penny Brown squealed just once, then she swept the legs from under Knuckles with a powerful swish of the brush.

A peculiar clippity-cloppity sound coming down the path turned out to be Penny Brown's mum galloping out of the house. She clapped her hands as if she was shooing pigeons.

"Penny! Penelope, stop that. What are you doing, have you people all gone mad?"

Mercifully, and at last, all hostilities ceased. When Knuckles picked himself off the ground, he was limping.

"Penny. Please tell me what is going on in this garden."

It was Shorty who spoke.

"Don't worry, Missus, it was only a friendly fight. Knuckles and Legweak were looking for Mabel, you see."

Mrs Brown surveyed the battleground which her garden had become. Potato plants had been flattened, the bristle head had come off the brush, fir cones lay everywhere and most of the rhubarb leaves were in tatters.

At last Mrs Brown found her voice.

"Look, I don't allow fighting of any sort in my garden. Penny, put down that brush this minute."

"He hit me in the face with a grenade."

Knuckles tried a pleasant smile.

"Not at all, Missus, it was only a fir cone."

"Shut up, you goat!"

"Penelope! Listen, you boys go home. I am very sorry but I will not tolerate this. If you want to throw things and break things do it in . . . oh my glory!" Mrs Brown stopped talking and stared at the rhubarb instead.

At first they thought that she was looking at an enormous dusty stone. But the stone moved. Lying under a leaf of rhubarb as big as an elephant's ear was an armour-plated creature – a design for living from two hundred million years ago, older even than the dinosaurs.

Mabel had not escaped into the golf course. Nor, indeed, had she been squashed by a lorry while slowly crossing the road. She had turned up alive and well in Penny Brown's back garden.

Jimmy Zest snapped into action first. Shorty dashed forward, too.

"Don't worry about the tortoise, Missus, I'll take care of it."

"Me too," shouted Knuckles.

But Mrs Brown caught each twin by an arm as they bustled past.

"I am not worried about the tortoise but I am worried about what is going to happen to you if you don't get out of my garden. Now! You too, Jimmy Zest, set down the tortoise and go home!"

They had to leave. She shooed them through the gate without further ceremony – and without big Mabel.

Knuckles was limping. The head of that brush had caught him on the knee. As the boys walked down the road, Shorty was suffering from another kind of pain.

"Oh, boy," he said. "Are we stupid. It must have been there all the time. Zesty – we should have looked under that rhubarb."

Jimmy Zest, Gowso and Shorty didn't dare call for Penny Brown the next morning. Instead they waited for her at the shops, hoping that she would eventually put in an appearance.

The boys had done some serious thinking overnight. It was Shorty who pointed out that nobody would have found Mabel if it hadn't been for the fight and they had an agreement with Penny Brown, after all. They had agreed on a five-way split if they found the tortoise, and fifty divided by five was ten quid each.

Legweak was there, too. He didn't want to miss the chat about the reward.

After Church, Penny Brown came to the shops for the papers. She had her best lemon-coloured suit on and she looked very smart in a straw hat with ribbons.

The boys gathered round Legweak's bike and waited for her to arrive.

"Penny," Gowso said as she went by, "could we talk to you for a minute?"

She stopped, turned, and came back. With one finger she exposed the face of her watch.

"OK, Gowso. One minute. Get out of my sight, Legweak. You broke my daddy's potatoes."

Legweak, banished, rode away to practise wheelies.

As she stared at the other three, Penny couldn't help thinking back to the events of last evening. Oh yes, Gowso and the others had got off lightly – not like her! She'd been forced to listen to a million reasons why you should never hit people with a yard brush – as if that snook Knuckles hadn't deserved it.

She was ready for them, all right. "What do you want, Gowso?"

Gowso couldn't face her. He looked to Jimmy Zest for help.

"We were just wondering, Penelope, whether you took Mabel back to Mr Hawthorne."

And Penny Brown smiled. She knew exactly what Jimmy Zest was fishing for. He wanted to hear about the reward.

"Of course I took her back, Zesty."

Actually, her mum had been with her, and she had refused to take any of Mr Hawthorne's money. He was a neighbour and Penny should be glad to help.

"Was he pleased?"

"Very pleased. Tears came into his eyes if you really want to know. He got out a bottle of olive oil and shined up her shell. He got Mabel when he was only twelve and he thinks she's seventy-five years old at least."

Penny glanced at her watch.

"Did you want to ask me something else, Zesty?"

He certainly did, but he knew she wouldn't tell him.

"No. That's all, Penelope."

Shorty, Gowso and Jimmy Zest watched Penny Brown go in for the Sunday papers.

"We should have looked under the rhubarb, you know," Shorty said again, with hindsight.

– 5 –

Warts and Witches

To keep a secret was a very difficult thing to do if you belonged to Miss Quick's class.

In fact it was almost impossible, for the pupils of Miss Quick's class were among the noisiest people you could meet. Gowso, Penny Brown, Legweak and the others missed absolutely nothing. Sweets in your pocket? They heard the paper rustling. A haircut? They made fun of your ears. They knew the date of every person's birthday and by half-past nine at the latest they knew what you had in your sandwiches for lunch and whether you had a goodie for break.

So, if Shorty hadn't wanted the class to know that his Aunty Sadie was a witch, he shouldn't have told Jimmy Zest and Penny Brown. He had only himself to blame.

It all started one day after school when Jimmy Zest said to Penny Brown that he could tie the laces on his shoes when he was only three.

"Boaster!" declared Penny Brown.

"You asked me, Penelope. You asked me what was the earliest thing I could remember."

"The earliest *important* thing. Laces aren't important, are they, Shorty?"

"They are if you trip over them," Shorty observed wisely as the three of them crossed the road by way of the patrol man.

There was a pause as Knuckles went by on the bar of Legweak's bike. Penny ignored the rude signs he was making and the conversation returned to what they had been talking about – their earliest memories.

"I was only four," Penny exclaimed. "It was the middle of a dark night and the wind was howling like a hungry thing. I stood up in my bed and turned my nightie inside out. That's *my* earliest memory."

It sounded very peculiar to Shorty. "What did you turn it inside out for?"

"To keep the witches away. They can't get at you if you wear your nightie inside out."

"There are no witches," said Jimmy Zest.

"Oh there *are*, Zesty," Penny said with conviction. "There's not as many as there used to be, but there are some."

Shorty, who wanted to say something to back

up Penny Brown, thought that Jimmy Zest had overlooked something.

"They didn't get her, did they, Zesty? She's still here. Maybe it works."

"*I'm* still here," said the sceptical Jimmy Zest, "and I wear my pyjamas the right way out."

"They wouldn't want you anyway, Zesty," snapped Penny Brown.

This piece of abuse had no effect on the imperturbable Jimmy Zest. After the three of them had walked the distance between lamp-posts in silence, Shorty gave them something to think about.

"My Aunty Sadie's a sort of witch."

Or so his dad had said. Aunty Sadie lived in a place called Jennystown Halt, near a river. To get to her cottage you had to go down a country lane and across a field full of swamps. Aunty Sadie wore her hair in a bun at the back of her head. It was supposed to reach all the way down her back when she let it out, like a rope, but Shorty had never seen it and he didn't believe hair could grow that long. She made wine in the autumn. His dad was afraid to drink it in case he poisoned himself and always poured it down the sink when he came home. He said it would kill all known germs and wipe out the rats. Aunty Sadie had once told

Knuckles and Shorty that she was boss of the birds and she was the only woman Shorty had ever seen sawing wood.

Penny Brown, meanwhile, had come to a complete stop and was staring at Shorty as if he had suddenly sprouted an extra head.

"A witch! A witch in your actual family? You're a lucky snook, Shorty."

However, Jimmy Zest was not so impressed. "How do you know she's a witch?"

"She talks to hens and cats."

"That's because she lives on her own."

"But they answer her back, Zesty."

They had now arrived at Penny Brown's house, where Mandy Taylor was waiting to play with Penny. Mandy wouldn't come over to hear the chat because she didn't like Shorty much and she wasn't too keen on Jimmy Zest either.

Shorty gave Penny her schoolbag, saying, "Don't tell Mandy about Aunty Sadie. She's a sort of a secret."

"Of course not, Shorty. Do you think I'm a gossip?"

Penny Brown deserted the two boys to go up her drive, whispering in Mandy Taylor's ear.

When Jimmy Zest got into his house he went straight up the stairs to his bookshelf and pulled out the volume of his encyclopedia labelled T–Z and hunted through the entries under W. There was over half a column on witches. One of the things he found out was that they used to burn witches at the stake. Jimmy Zest couldn't help smiling. If Aunty Sadie *was* a witch, it was quite a coincidence that her two nephews were the finest builders of bonfires in the country.

In school the following morning, people only wanted to talk about one thing. There was almost a fight about it. Gowso and Legweak got into an argument with Mandy Taylor and Penny Brown.

"Well go on then," Penny Brown said aggressively to Gowso – she was close enough to eat the nose off his face – "you ask him. You just ask him!"

She meant Shorty. And in fact it was Mandy Taylor who walked right up to Shorty and put him on the spot.

"Is it true that your Aunty's a witch?"

Shorty was a bit embarrassed, for they were all gathered round and waiting for his answer. He felt like the last pea on an empty plate. And Gowso was already scoffing.

"Well? Is she or isn't she?"

"My dad calls her an old witch," said Shorty.

This answer made Gowso turn right round to Legweak.

"See? It's just a nickname. How would his dad know if she was a witch?"

Penny Brown jumped in to tear this argument apart. "Because he's her relation, you snook. If you were related to a witch wouldn't you know?"

"Maybe, if she's a witch," said Mandy Taylor, "she could turn me into a frog."

She shouldn't have said that. Not with Knuckles standing right beside her. "It wouldn't take much to turn you into a frog," he said, "you're half frog already."

Then Knuckles mentioned the birds. He said that Aunty Sadie had a shed piled to the rafters with wood which the birds had brought to her. Sticks. They brought her stacks and stacks of sticks.

"They do not!" said Penny Brown.

She had the eyes of a believer – big and round and staring. She could picture mighty eagles and ugly crows and tiny little sparrows flying across the sky with sticks in their beaks for Aunty Sadie. Knuckles licked two fingers of his left hand and drew a huge cross over his heart.

"It's the truth. Shorty and I have seen them, haven't we, Shorty?"

"Yip. She's boss over the birds."

Now Penny Brown turned her attention to

Jimmy Zest, who hadn't said a single word about all this. "How do you explain that, Zesty?"

"I don't know."

"Only a witch could be boss over the birds."

"There are no such things as witches, Penelope."

Oh! she got fed up with him sometimes. He wouldn't admit *anything*. If only there was a way to prove him wrong, the snook, just once.

Shorty, meanwhile, had climbed up on a chair to shout at the top of his voice, "And another thing: my aunty Sadie can charm away your warts."

This was the moment that Miss Quick chose to come into the room and in a very short time she had charmed Shorty down from the chair with a couple of her special roars. The room went silent as Miss Quick steered everybody into their desks with deadly stares.

Every night, Mandy Taylor brushed her hair for two full minutes. The first minute was to make sure that the creepy-crawlies didn't pick *her* head to come and live in; the second minute was to make her hair shine.

And it did shine. She had nice hair, people often admired it, but how she wished it was black – jet black. If Miss Quick gave marks for hair instead of sums and stories Mandy knew she would only get eight out of ten. Maybe even only seven. If it was black she would be sure to get ten out of ten.

As she lay in bed feeling not yet tired, Mandy wondered about the rest of her. Her face, she decided, was worth only six because in her opinion it was spoiled by freckles. On the other hand her ears simply had to get ten out of ten. Hidden away behind her hair they did their job perfectly without any fuss or bother and no fault could be found with them.

Her hands were a disgrace. She had two-out-of-ten hands, it was dreadful. Her hands were covered with warts.

Well, maybe not *covered*, exactly. She had two on one hand and four on the other including a whopper on the outside edge of her thumb. She was ashamed to take anybody by the hand. And she'd tried all the remedies for the horrible things. She'd bathed them in onion juice and dandelion milk and her mother had bought brown stuff in the chemist's to burn them away. But she still had her warts.

Mandy Taylor lay in bed wondering about the Alexanders' Aunty Sadie. Was she really boss of the birds? *Could* she charm away warts? Quietly, she peeled back her continental quilt, tiptoed downstairs, and rang Penny Brown's number.

*

113

On Friday evening, Mandy Taylor and Penelope Brown waited for Shorty Alexander to come to the shops for his father's evening paper.

Unfortunately, Knuckles was with him, but the girls decided it couldn't be helped. They went ahead with their plan and bought Shorty a hamburger. Of course it had to be divided, and of course Knuckles gave Shorty the small bit.

Penny Brown started the conversation, "Shorty. Would you take us to see your Aunty Sadie? She could cure Mandy's warts and do weird things that would sicken Jimmy Zest. Please say yes, Shorty."

Shorty was standing there with his teeth in the hamburger she'd bought him. Penny felt he could hardly say no.

"What do you think, Shorty?"

"Dunno. She doesn't meet many people."

"Oh please," said Mandy Taylor, "you could write to her and tell her you want to bring some friends for a day in the country."

Knuckles gobbled the last bite of hamburger and licked his fingers.

"I'll take you," he said.

"We'll both take you," said Shorty, "but she's fierce. One wrong word and she takes a swipe at you with a stick out of the hedge. And she's not fussy where she hits you."

For a moment, Mandy Taylor dithered. Aunty Sadie sounded like an elderly Knuckles. Then she thought of her warts, and even smiled at Nicholas Alexander.

Every break and dinner time there seemed to be another story about Aunty Sadie. She not only cured warts – she told fortunes as well. It was said that the postman crossed himself after he put letters under her door. Gowso swore that Knuckles told him that she plaited her hair and let the cat climb up it. According to Mandy Taylor, Legweak said that she made dolls and cooked them in the fire and made people feel pain – though Legweak denied that he ever said any such thing.

With stories like these flying around there were naturally a lot of people keen to go on the trip. Aunty Sadie had become a tourist attraction. Legweak and Gowso managed to get invitations, though it cost them a couple of bags of crisps each. As the day of the trip came closer, Mandy Taylor warned her warts that they were on their last legs, and the thought of seeing a real live witch in the flesh made Penny Brown turn her nightie back-to-front as well as inside out.

And she had a warning for Jimmy Zest.

"If she is a real witch, you'd better admit it, Zesty."

"There are no real witches, Penelope," said the infuriating Jimmy Zest.

When the day arrived at last, the seven of them caught the ten-thirty train for the half-hour journey into the country. Five of them had a packed lunch with them. Knuckles and Shorty were relying on Aunty Sadie to make them sandwiches when they arrived.

Penny Brown was all nerves during the train journey. This was the first time in her life that she'd been on the same train as Knuckles and there wasn't even a teacher present to take the responsibility if he caused a disaster. But she got a very pleasant surprise. His eyes never once strayed to the emergency handle, and he only got up out of his seat to point out interesting places like the level crossing where a car had been sliced in two by a passing express. Just in case though, Penny and Mandy kept feeding him sweets from their tubes of Smarties.

Soon it was possible to look out of the windows and see only fields. Human life, it seemed, had disappeared, leaving just cows. They all cheered like mad when the train beat a bus to the end of a long, straight road and it seemed no time at all before the journey was over and they were all piling out on to a platform where the sign said: JENNYSTOWN HALT.

Legweak said he wouldn't have been surprised by a sign saying MIDDLE-OF-NOWHERE.

Knuckles, with Gowso at his elbow, led them over a footbridge into a lane. They had half a mile or so to walk, so Shorty stayed with Penny Brown and helped her with the bag which contained her lunch, Mandy's lunch, and both their flasks. Legweak brought up the rear with Jimmy Zest, who explained that the clouds overhead were cumulonimbus, therefore they could expect rain.

After a while Knuckles left the lane and cut across the fields. In the distance they could see the roof of a cottage and beyond it the long bend of a peaceful looking river.

Penny called out to Knuckles, "What time did you tell your Aunty we'd be there?"

"I didn't tell her any time," said Knuckles.

Mandy Taylor stopped walking. "Does she know we're coming?"

"I didn't tell her, did you, Shorty?"

"I haven't seen her since Easter," said Shorty.

"But . . ." Mandy Taylor stared in horror at Penny Brown. "Didn't you write, didn't you phone her? We can't just . . . *arrive*." She appealed to the others. "Can we? Not seven of us.

My mother expects people to phone or something before they drop in.

The Alexander twins had no time for the peculiar habits of the Taylors.

"Aunty Sadie hasn't got a phone," said Knuckles.

"She hasn't even got running water," said Shorty.

That settled that. Mandy Taylor had no choice but to go with the others, and shortly they were met by a border collie with a very busy tail. His ears flattened with pleasure as the twins made a fuss of him. It was Shorty who introduced him.

"The dog. His name is Glanpacker."

"I hope Aunty Sadie is as pleased when *she* sees us," moaned Mandy Taylor.

Legweak muttered that Glanpacker was a funny name for a dog. Knuckles replied that Legweak was a funny name for a human being. Then they saw the cottage.

It was a long, low building with small, stubby windows on either side of the front porch. The most remarkable thing about it was the roof. In the decaying thatch a number of weeds and wild grasses had taken root and grown.

"She's got nettles on her *roof*!" Gowso announced, dumbfounded.

"Over there," Shorty pointed, "that's where she keeps her wood."

They saw an open shed with no door. In the middle of the floor was a heap of twigs as big as an elephant. Every one of the twigs was as dry as a bone. Jimmy Zest walked into the shed and drew out one of the sticks and measured it. "Twelve centimetres. Did the birds bring all these?"

"Yip," said Shorty "Every one."

A very satisfied Penny Brown saw Jimmy Zest shaking his head in amazement. And truly, it was amazing. Even Knuckles and Shorty couldn't put together such a bonfire of thin and brittle little twigs. Penny shivered with excitement.

Knuckles scattered the hens in the yard as he walked forward to rap on the cottage door. The others stood by in a semi-circle wondering what to expect. Then Aunty Sadie appeared.

Penny just couldn't help staring. She had never seen a person wearing at least three layers of jumpers and cardigans before. Legweak thought it odd that someone so old and shrunken could be just an aunty. A granny, yes: but an *aunt*? Gowso felt very embarrassed because nobody was doing any talking, so he bent down to fiddle with Glanpacker's ears. He had a view of a pair of thin ankles disappearing into a pair of boots which looked as if they'd been in the army at one time. Jimmy Zest

studied the woollen hat on Aunty Sadie's head and thought that there wasn't much room under it for a roll of hair that could be climbed by a cat. As for Mandy, she thought that Aunty Sadie looked very fierce. And she was very disappointed to see a wart on Aunty Sadie's chin. Surely if she could cure warts she wouldn't have such an awful one of her own.

Aunty Sadie spoke suddenly, "Where did you all come from?"

Jimmy Zest stepped forward. "We came by train, Miss . . . eh . . ."

"What did you all come for?"

This was a more difficult question. Nobody was prepared to say they were here because they thought she was a witch. Penny began to search through her bag.

"My mum sent you a packet of tea, Aunty Sadie."

"I might not drink tea, did you think of that?"

"Oh. Oh dear. Well, I thought, she thought

. . . everybody likes tea."

"*I* don't like tea," Gowso blurted out.

Aunty Sadie scowled at her nephews – or rather, her great-nephews, for she was really their dad's aunty – and said, "This is your doing, you pair of devils."

Shorty didn't try to deny it. He said frankly, "We brought warts for you to get rid of."

Aunty Sadie gave a grunt and led them into a small room where the heat from the wood fire could be felt in every corner. The roof was so low that Gowso, who was very tall for his age, had to duck under a dangling oil lamp.

"Get up!" Aunty Sadie snapped at the twins. "There's not enough seats to go round so you pair can stand, serve you right." She hit the logs on the fire a vicious kick with the heel of her boot and sent a shower of sparks darting up the chimney. Then she sat on a hard-backed chair and looked at her visitors again.

The gallant Jimmy Zest rose from a soft chair. "Would you like to sit here, Miss . . . eh?" The trouble was, he didn't know what to call her.

"I would not," came the sharp answer. "Soft chairs for soft people."

Penny Brown almost smiled. But she was afraid to in case Aunty Sadie insulted her next.

Then a hen came waddling into the room through the open door and jerked its head about as if it was counting the people.

"Ah dear," said Aunty Sadie, "there's me old chucky hen in to see what the fuss is, aren't you, me pet? Yes. Duk-duk-duk-daak, duk-duk-daak."

Penny swallowed. She was thinking how she would die if the hen answered back – when it *did*. "Duk-duk-daak."

Glanpacker's ears pricked up too, as if *he* could understand.

"Aunty Sadie," said Shorty, "let down your hair and show them how long it is."

"I will not indeed," said Aunty Sadie. "Do you think I'm a peep-show?"

"Show them how you can find water with a bit of stick."

"I will not."

"Well show them something. We told them you could do weird things."

Aunty Sadie made a queer laughing sound as she stood up. "Which one of you has the warts?"

Mandy Taylor wanted to shrink away to nothing.

"I've got warts," she squeaked, "but so has Legweak."

"I have not," said Legweak.

"You have so, Legweak." This was Penny Brown to the rescue. "You've got a verruca on your left foot and they're the same only worse."

"How are they?"

"You can't go into the swimming pool with verrucas."

"Vurruc*ae*," corrected Jimmy Zest.

"Out!" roared Aunty Sadie, pointing to the twins, "out you go, take the dog down to the field and put up rabbits. Go on. But not you two!"

She didn't allow Penny or Mandy to leave with the boys. Instead, when the others had gone, she put out the hen and closed the door tight – to keep in the heat, she said.

And Penny Brown nearly died. In a corner, under an ancient old mirror, she spied a broomstick! Oh! she felt like something out of a nursery rhyme. What if Aunty Sadie really was a *witch*? But there was one good thing at least – Mandy didn't seem a bit afraid.

With brittle fingers, Aunty Sadie lifted a book from its place behind an old chiming clock. It was a dusty old book, exactly what you'd expect a book of spells to look like; and her eyes were misty with age as she passed a photograph to Mandy. "Hard to imagine, girls, that I was your age once."

Time had faded away the best of the detail from the old, brown photograph, but Penny and Mandy could still make out a girl of their own age standing in a garden of flowers.

"U-huh," said Aunty Sadie, nodding at them, "the girls never wore trousers in them days. They certainly did not."

"Well what *did* you wear?" asked Mandy – and soon they were chatting away about fashions and about the olden days, and about what a funny thing time was to bring so many changes.

Penny had a question. "Is it true what Shorty says – does your hair really reach the ground?"

"Not at all!" snapped Aunty Sadie. "It reaches down my back a bit."

"They said the cat could climb up it."

"Listen, those two say more than their prayers. What else did they tell you?"

"That you charm warts and tell fortunes."

"Dear bless me, only for fun."

"And," said Mandy, "they said you were boss over the birds."

This made a grin spread over Aunty Sadie's cracked face. Penny thought it was quite shocking to see what age could do to your teeth when she saw Aunty Sadie's four big yellow stumps.

"Come with me, and I'll show you something."

She led them down a quaint hallway with an up-and-down stone floor. It was as if so many feet had walked this way that the stone had been worn down in places. Penny and Mandy found themselves in another room.

"The parlour," Aunty Sadie said, "this is the good room."

And it looked terrible. One big rug covered the floor in the centre of the room – just as well, for there were actually holes in the floor at the edges of the room and one of the chair legs had poked right through. The fireplace just made Penny gasp. There were sticks in the hearth, sticks in the grate, the very chimney was blocked with sticks – right to the top, Aunty Sadie said.

"It's the birds, you see, they never learn. They start a nest in the chimney and the sticks fall down. So they bring more and more, the stupid things, and they fill that chimney every year. I'll have to get a bit of wire for over the top of it. 'Boss of the birds' indeed! Now come on. Us women will bake some scones before those children come back."

There was only one train back to town from Jennystown Halt that day, and it left at half-past four. While Jimmy Zest and the others waited for the train to arrive, they discussed all kinds of things about the visit to Aunty Sadie's – her warm, home-baked scones; Glanpacker's ability to put up rabbits; whether you could actually grow a crop of potatoes on your roof. This was Gowso's idea and it was scorned by everybody else. As the train arrived noisily, Mandy Taylor and Penny Brown were quietly swearing a vow of secrecy. Never, they swore, would they reveal to the boys the true length of Aunty Sadie's hair, though they agreed that it would be OK if Penny put it in her diary.

Sam McBratney

JIMMY ZEST

Jimmy Zest is such a pest!
He *loves* school,
is friends with *girls*
and is *always* right.

Well, right except for when his plans go wrong. And
that happens quite often, landing him and his friends in
all sorts of trouble. But whether they're dealing with
dinosaurs, worrying worms, testing strong stomachs or
examining aliens, they're never far from a funny
adventure.

The first collection of cracking Jimmy Zest stories.

'Created with great skill and humour' *Telegraph*

Sam McBratney

JIMMY ZEST, SUPER PEST

Jimmy Zest is such *trouble*. He just can't seem to learn that his plans *never* work out. That doesn't make him give up on them, though, which is something that *really* annoys his friends.

Mind you, they still join in as pesky Zesty causes chaos in a castle, troubles two teachers, runs riot with a rat and goes on a fishy expedition.

The *third* collection of cracking Jimmy Zest stories.

Sam McBratney

JIMMY ZEST IS BEST!

Jimmy Zest is just too *clever* for words. he can outsmart his friends and *sometimes* he can even outsmart his teacher. But that doesn't mean he's always *right* . . . not that he would agree with that.

But Jimmy Zest is at his best when he and his all-star friends do some funny fishing, have a run in with a white elephant, fall foul at a football match and cause cooking chaos.

The *fourth* collection of cracking Jimmy Zest stories.

Giants of the Sun

An anthology of Irish writing

Edited by Polly Nolan

A brilliant book bursting with spooky shipwrecks and smiling giants, dark tunnels and burning houses, tricked teachers and sparkly seasides, strange aliens and odd things in puddles.

An explosion of super stories from Ireland's very best writers.

Walter Macken

Flight of the Doves

Desperate to escape their vicious uncle in London, orphans Finn and Derval Dove embark on a dangerous journey across England to Ireland. Lonely and scared, their only hope lies in reaching the Connemara cottage of their beloved grandmother.

But for some reason their uncle offers a reward for their return and suddenly Finn and Derval find themselves at the centre of a nationwide search. Dogged every step of the way by people they don't know, who can the children trust . . . and how far will their uncle go to stop them reaching safety?

A classic Irish children's book.

A selected list of titles available from Macmillan Children's Books

The prices shown below are correct at the time of going to press. However, Macmillan Publishers reserve the right to show new retail prices on covers which may differ from those previously advertised.

SAM McBRATNEY

Jimmy Zest	0 330 39986 1	£3.99
Zesty	0 330 39987 X	£3.99
Jimmy Zest, Super Pest	0 330 40047 9	£3.99
Jimmy Zest is Best	0 330 40048 7	£3.99

All Macmillan titles can be ordered at your local bookshop
or are available by post from:

Book Service by Post
PO Box 29, Douglas, Isle of Man IM99 1BQ

Credit cards accepted. For details:
Telephone: 01624 675137
Fax: 01624 670923
E-mail: bookshop@enterprise.net

Free postage and packing in the UK.
Overseas customers: add £1 per book (paperback)
and £3 per book (hardback).